'You live alone, then?'

'Yes—I prefer it.'

'That proves you're quite grown up,' he considered. Had he doubted it? 'Only the truly mature can bear their own company for long periods of time.'

Heavens, she thought. From merely grown up to fully mature in just two sentences. In another minute, he'd have her right over the hill! 'I certainly hope I'm grown up,' returned Sheena. 'A twenty-six-year-old teenager would be an awful irritation, don't you think?'

Suddenly Dr Driscoll smiled, transforming his severe, fine-drawn face into something really quite attractive. 'I couldn't agree with you more,' he said. 'And, as there are far too many of them about, that could be why I prefer to treat juveniles. Well, don't be burning the midnight oil, Miss Scott. I intend to do a round of the nursery children tomorrow morning and I shall want you at your best for that!'

Drusilla Douglas is a physiotherapist who has written numerous short stories—mainly for Scottish-based magazines. Now the luxury of working part-time has provided her with the leisure necessary to embark on novels.

Previous Titles

SURGEON'S DAUGHTER
A SERIOUS CASE OF CONFUSION

PROBLEM PAEDIATRICIAN

BY

DRUSILLA DOUGLAS

MILLS & BOON LIMITED
ETON HOUSE   18–24 PARADISE ROAD
RICHMOND   SURREY   TW9 1SR

First published in Great Britain 1991
by Mills & Boon Limited

© Drusilla Douglas 1991

Australian copyright 1991
Philippine copyright 1992
This edition 1992

ISBN 0 263 77523 2

Set in 10 on 11½ pt Linotron Times
03-9201-54944
Typeset in Great Britain by Centracet, Cambridge
Made and printed in Great Britain

CHAPTER ONE

'THERE were, but now they've narrowed it down to three,' said Annie.

Sheena shared a knowing look with Betty. 'Trust you to know what's going on,' she teased, getting up from her desk to make coffee when the kettle boiled with its usual fuss and splutter. 'How *do* you manage it?'

'By virtue of my position,' Annie retorted with dignity. 'If you were the receptionist taking all the phone calls and running about with messages all day then you'd be the one in the know.'

'Nothing to do with sheer curiosity, of course,' was the clinical psychologist's sly suggestion.

Annie howled in outrage. 'If that's supposed to be a professional assessment, Dr Moira Cantlay, then I don't think much of it! Anyway, who is it keeps asking me if I've heard the latest?'

They all laughed, and Sheena said, 'She's got you there, Moira.' She passed round the mugs before resuming her seat and the previous topic. 'If they've pruned the short-list that much then we'll probably know who's to be our new director before the afternoon is out,' she guessed thoughtfully.

'All I'm hoping for is somebody half as nice as dear old Dr Ferguson,' said Betty, but they all agreed that was absolutely too much to hope for.

Dr Ferguson, the recently retired director of the Craigstoun Child Development Centre, had been loved as much as he was respected, and all the staff were feeling a real sense of loss. The rest of the lunch-hour was given over to appreciation of his skill and kindness, along with rather pessimistic estimates of the future. Moira summed up everybody's feelings when she said that the newcomer would have a great deal to live up to.

'Let's give the new boy or girl a chance,' Sheena urged at last. 'After all, we might get somebody who'll want things to go on exactly as they are.'

This prompted a chorus of derision, after which Moira said with a sigh, 'You'd not have said that if you'd been here when the candidates were looking round. They all had faults to find.'

'In that case, I'm very glad I was away on that course, because I mean to keep an open mind,' Sheena returned firmly. 'Now, girls, I don't want to hurry you, but——'

'We can take a hint,' responded Annie, leaping to her feet, 'Will you be in your room later on, Sheena? If so I'll give you a buzz as soon as I hear anything.'

'That depends. Betty and I have some planning to do before I go over to the hospital to treat wee Bobby Burns, but I have to be back by three to see a new patient. So I should be here until half-fourish, when I'll be talking to the mothers' group.'

The next half-hour or so was spent re-planning the physiotherapy programmes of children who were improving; then Betty, who only worked part-time, went home, and Sheena hurried over to the hospital. When she returned her new patient was waiting.

The next hour followed the usual course: putting the anxious mother at ease, making friends with the child, choosing suitable toys and then playing with him to learn as much as she could about his movement diffi-culties, before lifting him on to the couch for the actual examination.

He was an engaging two-year-old, already showing a charm that would give the girls something to think about twenty years on, as Sheena remarked to his mother.

'Do you see him leading a normal life, then?' asked Mrs Duff, clearly somewhat surprised.

'Goodness me, yes! His problems are the kind that he will adapt to and minimise as he grows. Don't expect him to be an athlete or a sportsman, but then how many of us are? He'll be more of a thinker, will this young man. There's a good intellect developing nicely under all those gorgeous golden curls.'

'That's what Dr Cantlay said. She said he was scoring like a three-year-old in some of the tests.'

'I can well believe that.'

The mother sighed all the same. 'If only we weren't so isolated, though. Y'see, Miss Scott, we're not Craigstoun folk. We come from Thurso and my husband's away a lot. He's a sales rep.'

'That must be hard, but Angus will soon make friends in the nursery—I'd like him to come daily for the first month or two—and you must join the mothers' group. There's a meeting later on today, if you'd care to wait.'

But this was a day when her husband would be home early for once, so Mrs Duff decided to wait until the next meeting. 'Meanwhile, if there's anything I can help with, please don't hesitate to ring,' said Sheena.

'You're very kind, Miss Scott.'

'We're here to help, Mrs Duff—Angela, isn't it? And I'm Sheena. We're all friends here.'

Having seen the Duffs away happier—Angus had enjoyed himself so much that he had had to be bribed with Smarties to leave—Sheena then settled down to record her findings. She had barely got started when somebody rapped imperiously on the door. As she had told Angela Duff, they were all friends together at the CCDC, so when nobody followed up the knock by coming in with a cheery greeting Sheena got up in some surprise and opened the door herself.

Her gaze connected with a well-cut jacket of dark blue. Travelling upwards via a spotless white shirt, Edinburgh University tie and a strong bronzed neck, it arrived at a lean, chiselled jaw, straight nose, piercing grey eyes under a slight frown, abundant light brown hair. . .

Before Sheena had finished her appraisal the man asked in a clipped Edinburgh accent, 'Miss Scott, senior physiotherapist?'

'Yes—that's right.' She had very nearly added 'sir', so authoritative was his manner. His look, though not actually disapproving, wasn't exactly flattering either. Sheena found herself tucking away a stray bronze curl and smoothing the collar of the bright flowered smock she was wearing over dark trousers.

'I wasn't sure. Your uniform—or lack of it. . .?'

'We don't dress formally here—uniforms frighten the children,' Sheena answered quietly. His manner was rather irritating—and who the hell was he, anyway? Yet another new administrator come to tell her she couldn't have the extra assistant she needed so badly?

'Quite so,' said the man, as though commending her.

What a nerve! 'Can I help you at all?' she asked rather more crisply than was usual for her.

'You can if you will tell me something about the set-up here. I'm Dr Driscoll—the new director.'

'Eh, wha——? How do you do?' returned Sheena feebly, putting out her right hand to have it just about crushed in a strong, cool grasp. The ringing of her phone was providential. 'Excuse me, please,' she said, retrieving her hand and darting over to her desk. 'Hello, yes?'

'The new man is on his way up,' bellowed Annie on the other end of the line. 'I'd have rung straight away, but somebody phoned me first.'

'Thank you, that'll be fine,' returned Sheena with great presence of mind, before hanging up on Annie's breathless supposition that the wretch was there already.

'Your intelligence system works well at any rate,' Dr Driscoll commented drily, letting Sheena know he had overheard Annie's trumpeted warning. 'I'll be sorry if that was the receptionist, though. I told her I preferred to announce myself.'

Useless to deny when Annie always shouted over the phone as if it couldn't be trusted to do its job unaided. 'I'm sure she merely wanted to make sure I was here—in case she had to institute a search, Dr Driscoll,' Sheena returned mildly.

'And where else might you have been, one wonders? The nursery and the treatment-rooms are empty. Could she have thought you might be having tea with the nurses?'

So the man had contrived to find everybody idle, had he? What rotten luck! Sheena took a deep breath and set about retrieving the situation. 'I am usually over in the hospital at this time, but, having had a new patient to assess today, I had to alter my schedule,' she opened firmly. 'I always make a point of treating myself any nursery child admitted to the wards. It's better for them to have somebody they know. And I like to go at this time so as not to steal time from the day patients, who are always away by now. We are very short-staffed,' she added for good measure. And, as by now it must be at least half-four, she had—with luck—got the nurses off the hook as well as Annie.

Sheena met look for level look and watched admiration dawning in Dr Driscoll's deep-set grey eyes. 'You should go into politics, Miss Scott,' he considered wryly. 'I have seldom heard a more spirited defence of position.'

Sheena awarded him a tiny smile. 'You did ask me to tell you something of the set-up, Doctor,' she reminded him in a voice like honey.

'But that was before I knew you were so pressed for time,' he returned smoothly. 'Perhaps there was something you were about to do. . .?'

When you found me idling away in here. Go on— say it! 'I was about to write up my findings on that outpatient I mentioned when you knocked on my door, sir.'

'The curly-headed charmer with the tiny, harassed-looking mother I met in the corridor, no doubt.'

A spot-on lightning assessment, Sheena applauded silently. 'The very one,' she confirmed.

'Then I am holding you up,' he decided. He was indeed, but he showed no sign of leaving.

'Not at all, Doctor,' politeness required Sheena to protest. 'I can easily take my paperwork home with me—I usually do, as it happens.' That was perfectly true, but Sheena hadn't intended to paint the picture of selfless dedication which, from his expression, he obviously suspected. 'I wonder what you will think of our assessment form?' she asked quickly, snatching one up and handing it to him.

He gave it several minutes of close scrutiny before saying, 'It is very comprehensive, Miss Scott. Who devised it?'

Sheena had, but she wasn't going to say so, so soon

after that scornful look. 'All the physios had sugges-
tions to make,' she returned woodenly.

'And how many are you?'

'Three—myself and two part-timers who help me in
the nursery in the mornings.'

'And your case load?'

'An average of forty children in the nursery at any
one time.'

'Then you are indeed understaffed,' he said roundly.

For an instant Sheena felt herself warming towards
him—until he added, 'At least for the kind of regime I
would wish to employ.' His tone seemed to suggest he
was not impressed by what he had seen and heard so
far.

Sheena's chin went up. 'I've visited quite enough
other centres to know that our regime is not universal,
so I expect you will make some changes,' she returned
evenly. 'So would it help your planning if I were to
give you a detailed account of how each therapist
spends her time?' She hoped he would say yes, because
such a list would highlight their desperate need for
another pair of hands.

'I couldn't possibly put you to so much trouble when
you have such a lot to do already,' he declined as
evenly, 'so please continue as you are for the present.
When I've seen for myself what needs to be done you
may be sure I shall let you know.'

Did it or did it not mean that his policy would be
one of 'do as you're told'? 'Thank you, Dr Driscoll,'
Sheena responded with a meekness that masked her
disappointment.

'Not at all, Miss Scott. You have been—most frank.'
And Sheena thought she had been so diplomatic!
'However, I'll not trouble you any more today.' He
regarded her with the same analytic scrutiny he had

accorded her when she had opened the door. 'I look forward to a useful working relationship,' he said drily before leaving.

Sheena knew that had been the merest formality. Clearly he hadn't taken to her any more than she had to him. It would be very interesting to hear the impression he had made on Moira Cantlay and Sister Innes. But that was for tomorrow. Now it was more than time to go and join the mothers. Always supposing they hadn't tired of waiting and gone home.

Seconds later Sheena burst into their cosy little club-room with an apology on her lips. 'Not to worry, Sheena,' said Connie Burns, who always acted as spokeswoman. It was her wee Bobby who was currently in hospital. 'Annie looked in to tell us you might not make it as you were tied up with Dr Driscoll.' Oh, Connie, how you do put things! 'So those who havena got anybody at home went off to be in time for the weans getting back from nursery.'

Inevitably they all wanted to know what the new director was like. 'Very businesslike,' Sheena returned fairly. 'And with so many candidates to choose from we may be sure he's right off the top of the tree. I think you'll like him,' she added. And so they probably would. At first glance she had been more than favourably impressed herself. Then, somewhere along the line, a note of discord had crept in. Sheena dragged her mind back to present matters. 'Now then, girls. Any problems?'

Amy Crockett wanted to know if her Jamie could have yet another pair of shoes built up. 'He wears 'em down that fast,' she sighed. Then Lyn Fairlie's mother thought that Lyn's squint was getting worse, so she supposed she'd have to go back to wearing that wretched eye-patch, and then Tommy Govan's mother despaired at length of ever getting him to use his right hand.

Sheena explained once again that a child with infantile hemiplegia usually did neglect the affected hand and then she suggested some more ingenious ways of tricking Tommy into using it. 'He's a full-time job, I'm telling you,' sighed the harassed mother.

'Like nearly all children with a physical handicap,' agreed Sheena sympathetically. She looked round quickly, making sure it was safe in this company to add, 'But you girls are among the more fortunate ones. Your bairns will all improve. I wish I could say that to every mum.'

'Sadie's wantin' to take her wee boy to yon place in Hungary,' said Connie, 'I felt like tellin' her that if you couldnae sort him then she'd be wastin' her time.'

Sheena sighed. The girls got a lot of support from each other, but there was always the danger that some such ill-considered remark would undo all the good. 'I'm glad you didn't, Connie,' she said. 'Dr Ferguson has told Sadie how extensive her laddie's problems are—and not to expect too much—but she finds it very difficult to accept. If he were my child I'd probably be wanting second and third opinions too, and I'm supposed to know all about these things. We must just let Sadie come to terms with this in her own way.'

There were murmurs of agreement from the others, while Connie muttered that one of these days she'd open her big mouth that wide she'd likely swallow both feet. 'Have a coffee, Sheena,' she said then, 'and let's talk about something else. How's your love life these days? Are ye still seein' yon guy from Perth wi' the Mercedes?'

Inevitably in this job you had to get a lot closer to your patients and their families than was customary if you were to win their confidence and be truly helpful. Sometimes that also meant revealing more about yourself than usual. 'On and off,' Sheena admitted, 'but Perth's a fair distance from Craigstoun, and I don't have that much free time, what with one thing and another.' And one of those things was definitely not for telling.

'You're not that keen, then,' returned Connie shrewdly. 'If you were you'd make the time, I'm thinking. What you're needin' is a change, so why d'ye no' come tae the disco wi' us some night? That's whaur I find ma men.'

'When it comes to the dancing I've got two left feet,' parried Sheena, glad to see that Mandy was now washing up the coffee-mugs: a sure signal that they were ready to leave. This conversation was getting out of hand. After all, wasn't she supposed to be the one dishing out advice?

Connie, it transpired, was planning to cram them all into her old banger and drop them off one by one. So, with nobody needing a lift, Sheena returned to her room to collect all those reports that never got written up in working hours; then she too set off for the car park, her mind busy with that final exchange. She had offered Mike and his Mercedes as a sop to Connie's curiosity, but no way could she have discussed David—the most worrying man in her life. He was drinking heavily again. Would he ever get himself together enough to put the past behind him and strike out in a new direction? Being struck off the medical register had been absolutely devastating—she understood that—but surely he couldn't continue much longer in his present aimless twilight of inactivity, letting the bitterness over what he had lost slowly eat him away?

Last time she went to see him she had risked

wondering aloud why he had made the sacrifice at all—
especially when he had been covering up for somebody
who wasn't even a friend. 'It's destroying you,' she had
said, hoping to jolt him back to reality.

He'd reacted all right, though not in the way she'd
hoped. First he had become incoherent and abusive,
and then he had hurled his copy of *Developmental
Paediatrics* at her. It was a massive book and it raised
a bump the size of an egg on her forehead, besides
almost knocking her out cold. 'Don't you ever say
anything like that to me again,' he had growled thickly,
impervious to her injury.

Sheena had left, vowing never to go near him again.
But she knew she would—just so long as he needed
her.

If Dr Driscoll hadn't side-stepped so smartly Sheena
would have walked right into him. 'From your
expression, it would seem that you have a very pressing
problem, Miss Scott,' he guessed.

Sheena shrugged off her preoccupation and apolo-
gised. Then, improvising, she said, 'Not mine exactly;
I've just been spending time with some of our mothers.
We meet regularly to discuss their problems and sometimes it's a bit—well, traumatic.'

'I'd have thought that was the province of the
medical social worker.'

'Yes, and Josie—Mrs Gordon—sees them regularly.
But, as so many of their queries relate to the children
and their progress, I got in on the act too.' In fact, the
mothers' group had been Sheena's own idea and it was
she who had got them their club-room, but she would
leave it for somebody else to tell him that. Naturally
she was hoping that somebody would.

He didn't tell her 'well done' as Dr Ferguson would

have, but transferred his gaze to her heavy load. 'Homework?' he asked.

'Yes. It's often easier to think and write at home. No distractions.'

'You live alone, then,' he surmised, sounding as surprised to hear himself saying that as she was.

'Yes—I prefer it.'

'That proves you're quite grown up,' he considered. Had he doubted it? 'Only the truly mature can bear their own company for long periods of time.'

Heavens, she thought. From merely grown up to fully mature in just two sentences. In another minute he'd have her right over the hill! 'I certainly hope I'm grown up,' returned Sheena. 'A twenty-six-year-old teenager would be an awful irritation, don't you think?'

Suddenly Dr Driscoll smiled, transforming his severe, fine-drawn face into something really quite attractive. 'I couldn't agree with you more,' he said. 'And, as there are far too many of them about, that could be why I prefer to treat juveniles. Well, don't be burning the midnight oil, Miss Scott. I intend to do a round of the nursery children tomorrow morning and I shall want you at your best for that.'

Abruptly he turned on his heel and strode off to a white Ford Sierra with the label of a well-known car-hire firm stuck to its rear window. Sheena stared after him. Appointed one day and starting work the next? No notice to be worked out? How very unusual.

CHAPTER TWO

SHEENA liked to get to work early. A quiet hour before the children were brought in, in the centre's own specially adapted minibuses, was vital for dealing with all the little things that got pushed aside once she started on therapy. Today Sister Innes was close behind her as she drove into the car park, and Dr Driscoll's hired Ford was already there. The girls had to pass it to reach the entrance, and Charlotte Innes said, 'Damn! I was so sure I'd be here before him. Did he sleep here, one wonders?'

Sheena laughed, glad to discover that she wasn't the only one whose feathers had been ruffled by the new director. 'If he didn't he was certainly still here at half-six. That I do know, because I almost knocked him flat on this very spot.'

Charlotte giggled. 'Was that not going a bit far, Sheena?'

'I didn't do it on purpose, you idiot.' Sheena became thoughtful. 'So what do you make of him, Charlie?'

Charlotte pursed her lips. 'He's not another Daddy Ferguson, that's for sure, but could be we'll have a better idea by the time he's done this morning's round. Oh, God!' She stopped short and grabbed Sheena's arm as they entered the hall and saw the new man answering the phone by Annie's desk.

'Leave it with me—I'll make sure she gets the message,' he was saying bitterly. Then he wrote something on the message pad, looking up as they approached. 'Good morning, Sister—Miss Scott. What time does the receptionist start work?'

'Eight-thirty' and 'Soon', they replied in unison.

One well-tailored eyebrow rose derisively. 'Strange that her boyfriend doesn't know that—or so many of the patients' mothers. That's the fourth call I've taken already.'

'We were promised an answering machine months ago,' said Sheena quickly.

'Meanwhile there is an obvious alternative,' he returned brusquely before stalking off towards his office cum consulting-room.

'Oh, dear—poor Annie,' breathed Sheena. 'I wish I'd thought of warning her to be prompt today.'

'I did, but you know Annie,' sighed Charlotte as they parted at the foot of the stairs.

Sheena and her two helpers, along with Moira, Charlotte and the nursery nurses, were all in the main nursery area when Dr Driscoll came briskly in at two minutes past nine. He seemed surprised at all the chaos and hubbub.

Those children already there were lying, sitting or standing—whichever came most easily—babbling and giggling as they struggled to remove their outer clothing with only minimal help from the staff. 'All part of the therapy,' said Sheena, stepping forward. 'But perhaps—just for this morning—we should do it for them, Dr Driscoll.'

'No—thank you,' he added as an afterthought. 'I am observing.'

The child he was observing was Dinah McCafferty. 'That small girl over there is scissoring. Badly,' he remarked severely, referring to Dinah's little legs, stiffly crossed, knees straight, as she tugged at her anorak.

'Oh, dear—she's supposed to be sitting astride on the train seat when she takes off her things,' breathed Sheena, darting forward, picking Dinah off the floor and planting the child astride her left hip to relieve the spasm. Then she looked round. 'Oh, dear,' she breathed again despairingly, 'Calum's got it. He's not usually on the first bus; I can't think what. . . We're very short of equipment, Dr Driscoll,' she stated, going over to the offensive in a stronger voice.

'And you are also without a carefully thought-out transport policy to take account of that,' he returned drily. But at least he had the grace to look apologetic when Dinah started bawling, upset by his unfriendly tone.

'There, there, my honey,' soothed Sheena, kissing the child. 'Nobody's cross with *you*.'

Ten minutes later, when Dinah had been pacified with a Jaffa cake and all the children were ready to begin their day, the round also began. 'Just you, Miss Scott,' said the new director, looking at the part-timers. 'You girls can carry on as usual. It will give me an opportunity to observe your methods.' Then he bent his attention on Sharon, who happened to be nearest.

She was kneeling at a low table, fitting shapes into a posting box, and Dr Driscoll stared at her so long and so hard that she sank to the floor and shuffled away on her bottom, saying, 'Bad man. Go away!' Not a happy start.

Sister Charlotte fetched her back. 'No, Sharon,' she whispered. 'Nice man, Nice doctor.'

Sharon listened politely before sticking out her tongue. She wasn't red-haired for nothing.

Sister then turned apologetically to the new boss.

'Her mother is over-protective,' she explained in a low voice. 'After her eldest child was molested in the park by a pervert Mrs Lindsay went right over the top, explaining at length to all her children why they mustn't ever speak to strangers. . .' She stopped in some confusion, and they all waited to see how Dr Driscoll would take that.

With a tiny grin he said mildly, 'But I'm not wearing a dirty raincoat, Sister.'

A titter from somebody at the back of the little group was soon stifled. They were all too unsure of him to laugh, and so his little joke fell flat. He suppressed a sigh and observed in an expressionless voice, 'Better over-protective than under.' Then he turned to Sheena to say, 'I like kneeling as a play position for children like Sharon with infantile hemiplegia, but that arm of hers. . .' He didn't need to continue when he saw the mounting flush on Sheena's cheeks.

'We usually splint it in extension for regular periods throughout the day, but Sharon takes her splint home with her and today her mother forgot to send it back.'

'Then improvise—no, don't tell me, you're very short of equipment,' he added before Sheena could answer.

Her mouth, usually upward-curving, went down at the corners and shrank to a thin, mean line. She was finding it very hard to keep that open mind she'd decided on the day before.

Dr Driscoll had moved on and was now earnestly comtemplating Michael McMahon. 'Is he not a big boy to be still in the nursery, Sister?' he asked. 'Why has he not been transferred to the special school?'

'It's miles away on the other side of town, sir, and his mother is a single parent who works right here in the hospital. So when we close here one of us takes him over to Paediatrics, where Sister McKenzie looks after him until his mother finishes her shift.'

'Very cosy and convenient,' considered Dr Driscoll in that dry way Sheena was beginning to think of as his 'I don't altogether agree with you' tone.

'And very humane too,' she muttered under her breath.

He turned and regarded her with narrowed eyes. But whether because he hadn't heard what she said, or because he had, there was no telling. 'Let me see how he is walking,' he said, sending Michael into raptures. He adored getting up on his feet and got very excited at the prospect. Unfortunately that increased the spasm in his leg muscles so much that he rarely did himself justice. 'A division of hamstrings might not come amiss here,' considered the director after a few more minutes.

'He has been on the orthopaedic surgeon's list for some time,' Sheena was glad to be able to tell him. 'But Mr Merryman likes the children to be able to walk at least fifteen yards before he operates, otherwise——'

'Well, of course,' Dr Driscoll interrupted in a long-suffering voice, putting Sheena firmly back where she belonged in his scheme of things. Somewhere between halfway down and the bottom of the heap, she decided grimly.

Sister intervened tactfully. 'This is our Tom, Dr Driscoll,' she said, bringing forward a plumply beautiful child who walked with a sailor's rolling gait, his feet well apart. 'As you can see, Tom has hypotonia and developmental delay, and when he came to us four months ago he couldn't even sit unsupported. The physios have done wonders with him.'

In fact, only Sheena had ever treated Tom and they

all knew it. Perhaps Dr Driscoll picked up the vibes prevailing, because he glanced at her briefly before saying, 'An extraordinary achievement, then; they have my congratulations. What methods were used?'

'Balance, compression and resistance,' Sheena returned curtly, while looking him straight in the eye. If he knew as much about physiotherapy as Dr Ferguson then that would be all the information he required. After that snub of his she had made up her mind to say as little as possible—at least, for the rest of that round.

The merest flicker of an eyelid was enough to let her know he'd guessed exactly what she was about. 'An admirable prescription,' he allowed smoothly. 'We must have an in-depth discussion about methods very soon, Miss Scott.'

Then, feeling two small arms clasped lovingly round his ankle, he looked down with a smothered exclamation of surprise. 'Now who have we here?' he asked indulgently as he bent to stroke the wee girl's curly head.

'This is Nancy—the nursery flirt,' said Sister, smiling.

'And what is wrong with Nancy, as if I couldn't see?' he asked in the same gentle tone. The slight nodding tremor of the pretty head was data enough.

'Ataxia,' said Sister and Nancy's particular nurse together.

Dr Driscoll flicked another slight glance Sheena's way as though expecting her to contribute too. She didn't. 'Similar methods to those used for Tom, perhaps?' he prompted.

'Yes—sir.'

'Nothing else?'

Sheena waited a second or two before saying reluctantly, 'We do play about a lot in front of the big mirror—sir.'

'Miwa—pitty Nancy,' said the child, who adored her own reflection.

'You seem to have found the right mix here, Miss Scott. For Nancy's ego, at any rate,' he added, cancelling the compliment.

'We aim to please,' retorted Sheena woodenly, forgetting her self-imposed speech embargo for the moment. His smile, quickly suppressed, suggested that it might have been worth it.

With question, answer and comment, the round proceeded. When it wasn't finished by eleven Sheena and Moira exchanged anxious glances. At this speed they would both end the morning with their work undone.

Dr Driscoll intercepted one of those glances. Had the man got eyes in the back of his head? 'This round is a necessary part of my initiation,' he said quietly. 'After this I shall see each child on the basis of need. However, I shall require to examine each one individually, so I hope you will all bear with me for the next week or so.'

There were, of course, murmurs of assent on all sides, and the rest of the round passed off without incident. By then there was barely time to treat one child before the nursery tables were set for lunch, so Sheena chose Angus Duff, the new child she had assessed the day before. Sharon had already taken him under her wing and Sheena was pleased, because their problems were broadly similar. Intent on showing off for Angus, Sharon joined in too, giving the lead in everything. Two for the price of one, thought Sheena gratefully. The morning had not been entirely lost.

As usual, Moira, Betty and Annie joined her in her

office for a snack lunch. Jane, the other part-time physio, always hurried home to let her nanny off duty.

All the girls were eager to give their impressions of the new man, but Annie, hotfoot and highly indignant from her private interview after the round, was given priority. 'That man is an out and out sadist!' she began, eyes flashing.

Psychologist Moira, who would only think of using that word in its proper context, looked startled. 'My God! Whatever did he do to you?' she breathed.

'Talked at me for hours—that's what,' claimed Annie. 'On and on about doing as I'm told——' She broke off and turned to Sheena. 'He heard what I said to you on the phone yesterday—and then there was a lot of stuff about having to do my job for me this morning. But I can't help it if folk ring up before I'm due in, can I? And so I told him!'

'I wish I'd been there,' said Sheena, dimpling. 'What did he say to that?'

'That I was to be in half an hour earlier in future. "Right," I said. "Then I'll be leaving half an hour earlier as well." Actually, that quite suits me,' Annie ended more mildly, before revving up again to growl, 'Pity he didn't stay in the US of A, say I.'

'Tell us more,' demanded Betty, voicing the general wish.

'He's been two years in some plush joint in California,' Annie began with relish. 'And he only got back last week. He's got some Yankee qualification as well as all the British necessaries. And he's written a book on developmental problems that will come out in the autumn.'

'Just how and when did you find out all that?' marvelled Sheena.

'From my friend in Personnel who processed all the

applications,' said Annie shamelessly. 'I gave her a buzz this morning while you were all dancing attendance on him. I used your phone, Moira, so there'd be no chance of being overheard again. By the way, he's thirty-three and single; not that that'll interest anybody here, when we're all fixed up, one way or another. When does your John get home, Betty?' she was reminded to ask, naming Betty's husband who was in the Navy.

Betty said hopefully in about six weeks, and so the rest of the lunch-hour passed in discussion of things less controversial than the new director.

'I'll stay on for a bit if you like, Sheena,' Betty offered when the group broke up. 'You couldn't have got much done this morning.'

Sheena confirmed that and accepted Betty's offer gratefully. They were fast making up for time lost when Annie came into the treatment-room to say that Dr Driscoll was asking for Miss Scott. 'Not to worry,' said Betty. 'I'll sort wee Peter as soon as I've finished stretching Calum's hamstrings.'

'You girls don't half sound cruel sometimes,' observed Annie severely as she followed Sheena out.

'What's it all about?' asked Sheena curiously, but for once Annie didn't know.

'He had Sister in his room for ages and then he told me to send you in next.'

'I see,' said Sheena, wondering if they were all to get a set-down in turn. So when she knocked on the director's door and was told to enter she did so warily.

Dr Driscoll was sitting at his desk, elbows on the arms of his chair and hands clasped over his diaphragm. 'Sit down, Miss Scott,' he invited, nodding towards the chair on her side of the desk. Not a reprimand in the air, then, or he'd have kept her standing.

'I have just seen a poor wee mite with a very rare and sadly fatal syndrome,' he said heavily.

With a sudden rush of sympathy Sheena realised that he was really upset.

'I've asked Sister to have her daily in the nursery, just to give the mother a much-needed rest, but I'm afraid there is little you can do for her, except perhaps to give some advice on positions for feeding, washing and so on. Baby Kelly Morrison has severe extensor spasm.'

'Does she also have convulsions?'

'Frequently.'

'Some evening baby-sitting too, then,' declared Sheena.

The new director stared at her as if she had gone out of her mind. 'I'm sorry, Miss Scott, but I really cannot see the connection.'

'Parents of such babies never manage to get out together because they're terrified to leave their child in the care of anybody without nursing experience—in case it has a fit and chokes. Never getting out together is very bad for their own relationship, so we've set up this service. All the nurses and physios are on the rota and we aim to give each couple an evening out about once a fortnight. There aren't many, so it's not too demanding.' By now Dr Driscoll was looking as if he couldn't believe his ears, so Sheena added defensively, 'It really helps them, sir—or so they say.'

'Altogether I have worked in six different paediatric hospitals, and this is the first time I've heard of such a service,' said the director slowly. 'It's way beyond the call of duty—and a wonderful idea.'

'I'm so pleased that you think so, Doctor.'

'Why should you have thought I might not?'

Now there was a facer. Because you haven't

approved of much else so far, was the retort that came first to mind, but Sheena actually said, 'As you pointed out, sir, it is an unusual service.'

He settled back a little more comfortably in his chair and continued his level scrutiny of her. Sheena wondered if he knew just how disconcerting he could be. 'Did I really?' he asked mildly. 'I rather thought I'd implied that it was unique and very praiseworthy.' After a slight pause he added slyly, 'You appear to have some receptive difficulties, Miss Scott. That must be a considerable handicap in your line of work.'

Sheena felt as though her cheeks were bursting into flame, and it was a long time since anybody—man or woman—had disconcerted her to such an extent. Don't bandy words with me, because you'll not get away with it, was the message coming over loud and clear. She stood up, gathered her tattered dignity and said a trifle unsteadily, 'I'll try to be more—more perceptive in future, sir.' She continued to stand to attention, waiting to be dismissed.

Having won that round, Dr Driscoll could afford to relent. His expression softened as he said, 'And I'm confident that you will manage it. Now I suspect that you're wanting to get back to your patients.'

'Yes—thank you, sir.'

He let her get as far as the door. 'Miss Scott. . .'

Sheena turned to see that the director had risen to his feet. Now he crossed the room unhurriedly and stopped in front of her. 'Everybody here is clearly on edge, and that is understandable, because Dr Ferguson ran this unit for a very long time and was greatly respected. But now I'm in charge, and since we all have our own ways of doing things there will inevitably be some changes. But none just for the sake of it, and none without discussion. I shall be obliged if you will convey that message to your colleagues.'

Why me, wondered Sheena, if my understanding is so deficient? 'I'll do my best, Dr Driscoll,' she returned quietly.

'Who could do more?' he asked as he opened the door for her.

Back in the nursery half the children were already into their outdoor things for the journey home, so that was the end of therapy for today. Betty had already left and Moira was talking to the parents of a patient, so it was Sister Charlotte Innes who was first apprised of the director's message. And she got it word for word, because Sheena had taken the precaution of writing it down while it was still fresh in her memory.

'One can't quarrel with that,' was Charlotte's first reaction. 'So maybe he's not such a bad lad after all. Certainly most of this morning's little hiccups could be put down to first-day nerves all round.'

'Could be,' allowed Sheena, while hoping that Charlie wasn't being too optimistic. 'Anyway, I'd better be getting over to the hospital now to treat wee Bobby, or Sister Smith will be thinking I've gone on strike.'

'How's he doing, Sheena?'

'Coming on slowly, but these respiratory attacks take all the stuffing out of him and he's got quite enough to put up with without them.'

'Whatever gave you the idea that life was fair?' asked Charlie as they parted.

It had been a long, hard winter but the air was gentle as Sheena set out for the paediatric block. Craigstoun General Hospital had grown up piecemeal around a mansion house, gifted long ago by a local industrialist. The Child Development Centre was housed in a no-frills post-war concrete building set in the furthest corner of the extensive grounds. Birds were singing in the tall trees now bursting belatedly into bud. From now on the walk to and fro would be a pleasure.

When Sheena reached Bobby's ward, Sister Smith met her in the corridor looking glum. 'A setback,' she said. 'He choked on a lump of carrot at lunchtime and it went the wrong way and got stuck. So he had to be bronchoscoped.'

'Oh, no, Sister.'

'Oh, yes, Miss Scott. He'll not be needing any chest therapy after the bronchoscopy, but all the upset has sent his spasm sky-high, as you might guess.'

'Poor wee pet—I'll see what I can do about that.'

Sister sniffed disparagingly. 'Not a lot, I should think. Anyway, he's still rather sleepy from the dope.'

Sister was on the brink of retirement, and, as she'd been nursing since well before physiotherapy evolved into its present modern form, she wasn't at all sure that she approved.

Sheena knew all that, so she said mildly, 'Still, he'll be expecting me, so I could at least talk to him for a moment.'

Sister shrugged. 'If you like—and, right enough, he has been asking for you. We've moved him into a cubicle for quiet.'

Bobby was lying with his eyes fixed on the open doorway. They brightened when they lighted on Sheena. 'Sheen—I fort you wasnae comin'.'

She bent over him and gently stroked one clenched fist. 'I couldn't let a pal down, now, could I?' she asked. Sister had been right about his muscle tone; it was up quite threefold on yesterday. So whatever had it been like before the injection? And fancy leaving him like this, with his skull pressing into this hard pillow! How many times had she let it be known that this was about the worst position for a child with such disordered muscle tone? Carefully she turned Bobby on to his side, rearranged his pillows and gently shook and stretched his wasted limbs.

Suddenly she sensed that somebody had entered the cubicle and, turning round, she saw Dr Driscoll watching intently. 'One of the nursery children?' he asked quietly.

'Yes—Bobby Burns. He's not a congenital cerebral palsy, though. He——'

'Ah got done by a bus when I wis four,' completed Bobby. 'But Sheena's gettin' us richt.'

'And how old are you now, Bobby?' asked Dr Driscoll in the gentle voice he reserved for the children.

'Ah'm six—well, a'most.' His eyelids drooped and he struggled to raise them again.

'He had a local anaesthetic not long since,' whispered Sheena.

Dr Driscoll looked puzzled. 'What for?'

'He had to have a bronchoscopy, which sent his muscle tone soaring.' Understandably that didn't relieve his perplexity. She was communicating badly again. 'Bobby choked on a piece of carrot at lunchtime and it got lodged in one of the main bronchi.'

'Is he dysphagic, then? Because, if so, his food should be liquidised.'

'No—it was a pure accident. He's been on solids and swallowing normally for some time.' Sheena looked down and saw that Bobby had fallen asleep in spite of himself.

Dr Driscoll was looking at him too. 'What a handsome child,' he said. 'But what I'd like to know is how a four-year-old happened to be in the path of an oncoming bus.'

'I'm not sure, Doctor—his mother gets very upset when anybody mentions it.' Her husband having gone off with another woman not long before the accident, Connie Burns had quite enough problems without getting another rocket. Besides, Dr Ferguson had read her the Riot Act at the time for letting Bobby play outside unsupervised. 'I don't believe there's any more I can do over here,' Sheena continued, 'so I'd better be getting back to the centre.'

Dr Driscoll followed her out of the ward. So whatever the business that had brought him there, it must have been completed before they met. 'Have you finished work for the day, then?' he asked as they descended the stairs together.

'Almost. Just a few reports and letters to write.'

'You call that "almost"?' he queried. 'It sounds more like a good hour's work to me.'

'Yes, it will be about that,' Sheena agreed. 'By the way, I passed on your message to Sister, sir.' She hesitated. 'Verbatim.'

A smile flickered over his face for an instant, before he returned gravely, 'Thank you kindly, Miss Scott.'

Sheena's home was a pocket-sized studio flat in a converted watermill, which sat beside a small river flowing through the heart of Craigstoun before going on to join the mighty Forth. When her friends in other places wondered how she could bear life in a moderate-sized industrial town with nothing much in the way of architecture or history to recommend it Sheena pointed out how convenient it was for Edinburgh, Glasgow and the splendid Perthshire countryside. Not to mention the tiny village where poor David had chosen to hide himself away after his career disintegrated.

On the way home she had been to the supermarket,

and now she put a pork chop under the grill before stashing away her groceries. A crisp roll, salad and fruit completed her meal, which she ate off a tray by the window of her only but fairly spacious room. She had just finished eating when she saw Mike parking his red Mercedes in the cobbled courtyard below. By the time he had climbed the three flights of stairs and rung the doorbell Sheena had washed up her dishes.

'Surprise, surprise,' he said when she opened the door. He was slightly out of breath, and for the first time Sheena noticed the merest suggestion of a paunch.

'What happened to the Wednesday squash?' she asked as he kissed her briefly on the cheek.

'I cancelled it. Put on your best bib and tucker and I'll tell you why over a spot of grub in the pub.' He often spoke that way—like somebody in an old movie.

'I've already eaten,' she said, 'but I don't mind drinking coffee while you do.'

'Great.' When Sheena had patted her shining auburn bob in the lobby mirror and picked up her shoulder bag Mike asked doubtfully, 'You're not really going out dressed like that, are you?'

Sheena glanced down at her plum-coloured corduroy skirt and matching sweater. 'Why? What's the matter with this?'

'Is it not what you've been wearing all day?'

Poor Mike! He had a horror of hospitals and would be thinking that her outfit was infested. 'No, it's not. Everything I wear at work is strictly machine-washable.' Her lips twitched slightly. 'Believe me, it needs to be.'

His lips curled in distaste. 'I should think we'll both be glad when you're outa that dump, doll.'

Sheena locked her door and clattered after him down the resounding concrete stairs, wondering what he was getting at. She didn't find out until Mike had tucked away a large steak and a mountain of chips. Then he lit a cheroot, blew a couple of perfect smoke rings—a skill of which he was very proud—and said calmly, 'I've got you a job in Perth.'

Sheena stared at him, thunderstruck. 'You've *what*?'

'I've got you a job in Perth,' he repeated. 'I knew you'd be pleased. A guy I know has a private practice and he's making a packet, with Perth being full of loaded old biddies who think they've got everything from dandruff to flat feet. He's badly needing an assistant and he's willing to give you a trial.'

Sheena slumped back in her seat, gasping soundlessly and hardly knowing where to begin. Meanwhile Mike went on and on, describing the delights that awaited her in the fair city. When he said, 'And you don't need to worry about finding a pad, because you'll be moving in with me,' she realised it was high time to interrupt.

'Steady on there,' she began, 'I know you mean all this most kindly and I appreciate it, but it's not quite that simple. I'm a highly trained paediatric physio and I love the work. I haven't treated adults with the sort of problems appearing in outpatient departments since I was a student, so I'd not have a clue about private practice. I don't think your friend will want me when he knows that.'

He didn't understand one bit. 'What's so special about treating kids?' he wondered. 'Surely once a physio, always a physio? As for the rest, Laurie'd soon teach you how to use all those shiny electrical gadgets that impress his clients so much.'

'I know fine how to give electrotherapy—it's part of our basic training—but treating children with neurological disorders calls for a specialist skill which takes years to acquire. I couldn't waste all that when there's such a shortage of paediatric physios. It would be—all wrong.'

'Don't you want us to be together?' he demanded incredulously.

Well, did she or didn't she? Sheena honestly didn't know. 'If it were a job working with children, then maybe——'

But Mike had decided to go on misunderstanding and to take offence as well. 'No need to make excuses,' he growled. 'Never mind that I've spent weeks chatting up this guy; persuading him what a boost you'd be to his business.' Business! Sheena could feel her own temper rising at that. 'If you prefer a pack of squalling brats sicking up and peeing all over you to a nice clean clinic job then you'd better stick with 'em!'

Mike hadn't troubled to keep his voice down and people around were watching and listening. It was very embarrassing—to Sheena, at any rate. 'Please try to understand,' she said quietly. 'I'm not being ungrateful, but there really is a world of difference between treating physically handicapped children and adults with arthritis and sports injuries and things like that. Such a change of direction needs a lot of thought. Can you give me some time?'

'Do I have a choice?' he grunted. 'But you'd better believe you're not the only one up for consideration.'

For the job of assistant to his friend Laurie—or live-in lover for Mike? 'Then I'll just have to take my chance, will I not?' asked Sheena with quiet firmness as she got to her feet.

'Just as you like,' Mike returned implacably. When they left the pub he elected to go straight home.

Sheena watched him drive away with scarcely a qualm and made her way back to her flat. They had

had disagreements before, none of which had really upset her. Which, now that she thought about it, told her quite a lot about the true state of her feelings for Mike.

CHAPTER THREE

HAVING told the minibus drivers the night before that, from now on, Dinah and Calum must be brought in different buses, Sheena went straight to the nursery next morning and looked round. Tom, Nancy, Peter, Sayeed, Johnnie, the Millan twins. . . 'Where's Dinah?' she asked the nearest nurse.

The girl was busy changing baby Dora's nappie. Looking up, she said brightly, 'Not here yet, I guess.'

'But both buses have brought their first lot and gone for the second. I saw them myself.'

'That's right, Sheena. Perhaps Dinah's ill or something.'

'Was there a message?'

'If there was then Annie will know.' Who else?

Annie's chair was balanced precariously on its two back legs as she sat with her feet up on her desk, staring moodily at the phone. 'Not so much as a bloody wrong number out of the thing this morning, and me in at the crack as per orders,' she grumbled. 'So much for Don Driscoll and his fancy ideas.'

'I didn't know his name was Donald,' said Sheena, momentarily diverted.

'It isn't—it's Matthew, and he's known as Matt. But I'm calling him Don as in Spain. You know—playing the laird, cock o' the walk, stalking about and cracking the whip.'

Sheena had to admit that it suited him, with his air of authority and the way he had of looking down that straight nose of his.

She turned away, hiding a smile. 'Just don't let him hear you, that's all.'

'I'm not afraid of him,' asserted Annie boldly. 'I can transfer to Outpatients any time I like. Anyway, he's got a clinic this morning, so I'm quite safe for the time being,' she called after Sheena as Sheena returned to the nursery.

Dinah arrived in the second wave—with Calum. Yesterday morning in reverse, despite Sheena's careful instructions. Satisfied that at least Dr Driscoll wouldn't find out, she parked Dinah astride the broad engine seat and encouraged her to pull off her hat. 'Go on, sweetie—arms up. Up, up, up to the sky——'

'Miss Scott, that child over there is scissoring badly!'

Damn, blast and every other swear word. 'But he's sitting in a chair with a pommel, sir,' Sheena retaliated as she scrambled quickly to her feet.

'I don't see any pommel.'

Sheena looked too. 'I suppose he must have pulled it out.'

'Has he done that before?'

'Now and again,' Sheena reluctantly admitted.

Dr Driscoll didn't need to reply; his expression was saying it all. 'After yesterday's mix-up I asked specifically that these two children should be brought in at different times,' Sheena said firmly. Now, of course, he'd think she was putting all the blame on the drivers. Which I am, she realised.

'I've always found that written instructions are more effective than verbal ones in matters of importance,' said the director in a voice of conscious patience.

'Thank you, sir—I'll remember that,' Sheena returned, outwardly calm, but inwardly seething.

'I came across in response to a message from Sister Innes,' he then revealed. 'Do you know where she is?'

'In the dressing-room with a child who has come in badly bruised, sir. Sister is very concerned.'

'So she gave me to understand when she phoned. Thank you, Miss Scott.' A pause. 'There is no need to call me "sir" all the time, you know.'

'Thank you, Dr Driscoll. It just seemed—appropriate.'

Apart from the slight lift of a well-tailored eyebrow, Matt Driscoll made no response; just walked away in search of Charlie.

After that unpromising start the morning settled down and pursued a more or less normal course. Sayeed hit Joyce on the head with his plastic hammer. Nancy painted her face instead of her picture, and Sharon hurt the window cleaner's feelings by calling him a dirty old man when he offered her a sweet. Tom actually tried to balance on one foot before he was asked to, Peter was sick, and Michael invited Sheena to bugger off when he thought he'd had enough stretching of his tight muscles for one day. Just the usual things.

While the children had their mid-morning orange juice and biscuits Sheena joined her assistants Jane and Betty in the kitchen for a quick coffee.

'They're putting wee Alan on the at-risk register,' revealed Jane. 'Dr Driscoll says there is no way he could have got those bruises by tripping over the dog, as his mother said in her note. If he'd done that he'd have fallen forward, and the bruises are all over his back.'

'I'm glad I'm not Josie,' breathed Sheena, naming the centre's medical social worker. 'She'll have to visit the home and probe around a bit.'

'Josie's very tactful.'

'All the same, they'll know why she's there,' guessed

Betty. 'How *can* anybody ill-treat a child, however tiresome?' she demanded fervently.

Sheena didn't try to answer. It was too complex a question and one that obsessed Betty. But then Betty, who adored children, had been married for eight years without managing to conceive. So Sheena tried to divert her by saying, 'Michael's going to see Mr Merryman again this afternoon. What's the betting he's admitted for division of adductors this time?'

'That reminds me,' responded Jane. 'I think my Darren ought to be seen too. The muscle pull is so strong that his right hip is bound to dislocate.'

'Then I'll take him along as well. It'll be all right, so long as I give Sister Stewart a buzz first.' Sheena set down her mug, still half full. 'In fact I'll do it now before I get started on therapy again.'

The children's orthopaedic clinic always started promptly at one and, as any nursery children were always seen first, Sheena left the lunchtime gathering in her office earlier than usual. 'And don't be leaving dirty mugs all over my desk,' was her parting shot.

Moira promised they wouldn't, and Sheena went to find their odd-job man cum porter. He was in his little hut for once, reading the *Sun*. 'There are two wheel-chair cases for Outpatients this afternoon, Hamish,' Sheena began. 'Could you possibly push one of them for me?'

'You might of told me,' he growled predictably.

'I did try, but you were at a union meeting. Did you not see the note I left for you?'

'No—I never saw no note.'

Useless to point to it, prominently displayed. With the Hamishes of this world, a large helping of soft soap worked better. 'Sorry about that, but if you *could* possibly see your way to sparing me ten minutes, I'd be *so* grateful. . .'

'I'm awfu' busy, mind, but I reckon I might manage it.'

'Hamish, you're a gem.' What an overstatement, but effective.

'Och awa', lassie. Onnyways, you're no' so bad yersel'.'

Mr Merryman's consulting-room was filled to capacity, what with his own considerable bulk, Sister Stewart, half a dozen medical students from Glasgow—and Dr Matt Driscoll. Sheena was surprised to see him; then realised that she shouldn't have been. Dr Ferguson had usually managed to attend if any of the nursery children had appointments.

Michael didn't mind the crowd one bit—he always enjoyed an audience—but Darren was completely overawed. Noting the quivering of his bottom lip, Sheena scooped him up in her arms for reassurance.

'Do I know that young man you're holding, Sheena?' asked the orthopaedic consultant, with whom Sheena was on excellent terms, having trained with his daughter.

'Not yet, Mr Merryman—we slipped him in at the last minute because his physiotherapist is concerned about his left hip.'

'The X-rays then, please, Sister,' he demanded, but Sister Stewart was already putting them up on the viewing screen.

'What do you see, then, gentlemen?' barked Mr Merryman at the students. Two of them were girls, but he wasn't bothered about such a detail.

Obediently they gathered round and gazed. 'Well?' he prompted after a silent second or two.

A lot of throat clearing, and then somebody offered truthfully, 'The bones are all in bits, sir.'

Mr Merryman exchanged looks with Dr Driscoll before asking patiently, 'Can anybody tell me why?'

'Age, sir,' they offered in chorus.

Another pause and then, 'Would anyone care to elaborate?' he asked.

'Because he's not yet ossified, sir,' said the one who had spoken first.

'Thank heaven for that,' returned the orthopod. 'He's not yet three and has a lot of growing to do first.' Then, perceiving rightly that they hadn't a clue about the problems of slow bone growth in cerebral palsy, he proceeded to give them a very clear account of the importance of weight-bearing in the development of stable hip-joints and how, when walking was delayed, the head of the femur did not always develop properly—with the inevitable tendency to dislocate. Especially when there was abnormal muscle spasm present as well. 'Congratulations to the physio who treats this wee lad for detecting this so promptly,' Mr Merryman instructed Sheena when he had finished examining Darren. 'What measures have been taken so far?'

'Cheyne-style padded pants for abduction and getting him to kneel as much as possible, sir.'

'Good lass, good lass. Sheena knows what she's about, Driscoll,' Mr Merryman was good enough to tell the new director.

'She certainly gives that impression,' was the impassive reply. Had he meant to imply that it was all a front with no substance behind it? I could get paranoid if I'm not careful, thought Sheena. But there was no time to dwell on that when Mr Merryman was already looking round for Michael.

As Sheena had surmised, the great man was now ready to operate. 'Why am I doing this?' he asked the students, going on to tell them whenever he saw their blank expressions.

'Let me get this straight, sir,' said the one who had stuck his neck out twice before. 'Cutting through his thigh muscles is going to help this boy to walk better?'

'I'm not proposing a total hatchet job,' returned Mr Merryman testily. He believed he had made himself perfectly clear the first time. 'But, when muscle tone is much higher in some groups than others, distortion and deformity is bound to occur. A division of fibres in the most affected muscles redresses the balance and allows a more normal gait pattern.'

The student was still looking unconvinced, so Sheena decided to escape before Mr Merryman called her the muscle expert and passed the boy over to her for further enlightenment, as he had been known to do when sufficiently exasperated. 'Thank you for seeing our two wee people, sir,' she interrupted hastily. 'Now I'd better be getting them back.'

From Reception she phoned for Hamish, who didn't answer. Sheena had expected as much but reckoned it was always worth a try. When she told the boys she'd have to take them one at a time Darren's lip quivered again, while Michael began his favourite 'it's no' fair' monologue. So Sheena rolled up her sleeves, so to speak, and set off for the centre, pushing one wheelchair and dragging the other.

When they had gone about twenty yards like that she heard Matt Driscoll asking from behind just why she was doing a porter's work. 'And I don't think that is a very safe procedure either, Miss Scott,' he added before she could explain.

Sheena sighed, stopped and turned to face him. 'Our

only porter was otherwise engaged.' Just wait until I get hold of you Hamish McTear! 'Neither child wanted to be left behind, and I've had to do this so often in the past that I could manage with my eyes closed,' she claimed crisply.

'Judging by the zigzag course you were pursuing, I rather thought they were,' he retorted even more crisply.

Sheena squared up to him, ready for battle. But, 'Not in front of the children,' Matt Driscoll reproved her maddeningly while loosening her grip on Michael's chair and expertly reversing it to face forwards. 'Isn't it a good thing I'm going your way?' he then asked slyly. 'Well, come along, then.'

He set off at such a cracking pace that Sheena could hardly keep up with him. In fact she was almost running by the time they reached the centre, what with Michael shrieking ecstatically, 'Dinnae let 'em catch us, Doctor,' and Darren begging her to get a move on.

When they arrived Annie was sitting at her desk, filing her nails. She dropped her emery board and stared at the sight of the new director pushing Michael's wheelchair, while Sheena, scarlet and dishevelled, followed with Darren. 'Would you take over now, please, Miss Crawford?' requested the director imperturbably. 'And then ask Sister if she will be good enough to bring Dinah McCafferty to my room.'

'Dinah gets the Peto class along o' me,' put in Michael, losing no chance to mix it as usual.

'All right, then, so who can I examine?' asked Dr Driscoll, fixing Sheena with a level look.

'Oh, really, sir,' she responded, flustered.

'I've no wish to disrupt the therapy programme as it currently stands, so how about Peter Paterson? I hardly think he's in that class if you follow the basic rule about having children of similar physical abilities together.'

'No, he's not, and yes, I do,' answered Sheena, peeved by his assumption that she didn't know to do that. She waited for another slighting comment on her poor powers of communication, but Matt Driscoll merely turned to Annie and said, 'Peter Paterson, then. Got that?' Then, satisfied that she had, he said, 'Cheerio for now, then, lads,' to the boys, before going into his consulting-room and shutting the door.

Annie scuttled off to do his bidding, while Sheena stared at that closed door. What an unpredictable man he was. Would she ever learn to read him right?

An outbreak of squeals and yells from the nursery brought Sheena scurrying at the double. As usual, it was a question of two children wanting the same toy at the same time, and a nurse was already separating the combatants. 'So much for Dr Cantlay and her free-association play period,' she grumbled when they had been placed at opposite ends of the room. 'When they're left to choose there's always a fight.'

'At least it gets them using their voices if nothing else,' soothed Sheena. 'No, Tom, don't shuffle around on your bottom like that. You can walk now.' She picked him up and set him on his feet with a sturdy wooden horse on wheels to push. 'Ready, steady, go. . .'

'S'quicker,' said Tom, giving her a long-suffering look before dropping to the floor again and shuffling off at the speed of light.

'You're never letting him away with that, are you?' asked the nurse, shocked.

Sheena shrugged resignedly as she watched him go. 'Every child rebels from time to time, I guess. Anyway, it's almost time for the class and he loves that.'

'Only 'cos he loves beating Sayeed with his baton, the wee monster.'

'So why do you think we've started putting them at opposite ends, then?'

'You've got to be fly at this job, I'm thinking,' responded the girl as they rounded up the children who would be taking part.

Just simple exercises; simple, that was, for a child with all his muscles and nerves in prime working order. And all the time the childish trebles chanting, 'We are going to lift our arms, we are lifting our arms. . .' Professor Peto had called that rhythmic intention. There was no doubt that an element of competition was sometimes very useful.

Sometimes, though, things didn't go so well. A tumble or two, a few tears, even a battle such as Nurse Forbes had sketched out between Tom and Sayeed. Today, though, all was harmony. And just as well, Sheena thought thankfully afterwards when she discovered Dr Driscoll propped up against the wall just inside the door, watching silently.

On reflection she had to admit it was probably his presence and not her own that had brought about such perfect behaviour.

'That seemed to go well, Miss Scott,' he considered. Only seemed? He should see them sometimes; then again, perhaps not!

'They love this session, Dr Driscoll.'

'Obviously.' A pause. 'It occurs to me that a group treated solely on these lines might be worthwhile.'

'The big snag would be the shortage of staff. We'd need another full-time physio to take charge of it.'

'Not the first time I've heard that particular objection,' was Dr Driscoll's parting shot.

He thinks I'm just making difficulties, decided

Sheena while she tidied up the room prior to going over to the hospital to treat Bobby Burns. He was so much better today that the registrar decided he could go home whenever his mother could collect him. However, one of the hospital physiotherapists was wanting Sheena's advice, so she got back to the centre even later than usual.

By then Annie had left, and the internal phone on the reception desk was ringing imperiously. Sheena picked it up. 'And about time too, Miss Crawford,' reproved their new director in a steely voice before Sheena could say anything. 'I have been trying to secure your attention for the past ten minutes. Will you please bring me the notes of Sayeed Aziz, Sharon Lindsay and baby Dora Dewar? Thank you.' Plonk went the receiver at the other end of the line.

Sheena replaced hers with a thoughtful little smile. Clearly he had forgotten readjusting Annie's working hours, and, as a result, Sheena could see her way to administering a delicate reproof. The director divided his time between the centre and the hospital. On those afternoons that Dr Ferguson spent here, it had been one of Annie's tasks to take a tray of tea to his room at four. It was now ten minutes after. Still with that impish little smile, Sheena went to the kitchen. She prepared an immaculate tray, and while the kettle boiled she collected those files Dr Driscoll had demanded. Finally she carried the lot to his room. Would he see the posy of polyanthus as sarcasm? Sheena rather hoped that he would!

Certainly there was no denying his amazement when she set the tray in front of him and carefully arranged the files beside it. 'What's all this, then?' he asked with less than his usual polish as he looked from Sheena to the tray and back again.

'Your tea, sir, and the case-notes you asked for.'

He laid a hand on the notes; a good hand it was, strong and square with well-shaped, well-tended nails. 'It was Miss Crawford I asked to bring these.'

'No, sir, it was I who answered the phone when I got back from the hospital.'

He frowned. 'So where the devil is that dizzy receptionist?'

'Halfway home, I imagine. With the change to her working hours, she now goes off duty at four o'clock.'

He digested that before asking, 'But why the tea?'

'Another of Miss Crawford's late-afternoon duties, sir. Dr Ferguson liked it.'

'Did he, now? Well, I don't recall asking for it.'

Sheena swallowed her chagrin at the backfiring of her little plan, and, picking up the tray, she headed for the door.

'Bring that back,' he ordered. Still without a word, Sheena obeyed. 'I said I didn't ask for it—I didn't say I didn't want it.'

'I'm sorry, sir.'

Matt Driscoll fixed Sheena with eyes that glinted dangerously. 'If you call me "sir" just once more in that provokingly long-suffering tone, I shall probably strangle you, Miss Scott,' he warned. 'Now listen to me. It was very kind of you to bring these files; for the moment I had quite forgotten rearranging Miss Crawford's hours. It was even kinder of you to bring the traditional tea. Now kindly fetch another cup for yourself, and when we are suitably lubricated we will see if we can hammer out a reasonable working relationship.'

'I have a lot of paperwork on my desk, sir—Dr Driscoll.' Sheena substituted quickly, not being particularly anxious to have her neck wrung.

'Quite the best place for it,' he countered impassively. 'Now will you please be good enough to do as I
asked?'

'I—I don't. . .' She'd been going to say that she
didn't want any tea, but quailed before his angry stare.
'Yes, sir,' she complied—and this time he'd have been
hard put to it to describe her tone as provocative. This
time it had been positively servile.

When Sheena returned with a second cup and saucer
Matt Driscoll was on the phone. He didn't look at her,
but signed for her to pour out. She did, leaving him to
take his own milk and sugar, since she didn't know his
preferences. Then she stood quietly by, waiting for him
to finish his call.

At last he replaced the receiver and regarded her
impassively. 'Do you always drink your tea standing?'
he asked ironically.

Sheena answered that by carrying her cup to the
remotest chair. It was quite a big room. Dr Driscoll
watched this performance with continued calm. Then
he said, 'I seem to remember observing on a previous
occasion that your decision to live alone denoted
maturity. Clearly I was too hasty in that judgement.'
He then got up and placed a chair beside his desk. 'I
have a distaste for shouted conversations,' he observed
as he resumed his seat.

Having lost the initiative so completely, Sheena
obediently changed chairs. Matt Driscoll was drinking
his tea and eating biscuits in perfect, unhurried calm,
while Sheena grew more and more uncomfortable. She
hadn't felt like this since she'd been called to the
principal's office to be reprimanded for some minor
breach of rules during her first term at college. When
suddenly he fixed her with a steady gaze she actually
trembled. 'Dr Ferguson was a fine man and a very hard

act to follow,' he began. 'Inevitably you feel regret at his retirement, but resenting his successor is not going to be very productive, is it?'

Sheena shook her head in silent agreement. But it wasn't that—not entirely. Yet how else to explain this strange feeling of inadequacy and hostility he evoked in her? And it would be most unwise to try!

'Both Dr Ferguson and Mr Merryman think very highly of you—both as a person and a therapist,' he continued. 'I should be very sorry if your attitude obliged me to do otherwise.' Was that a threat or a warning?

'So would I, Dr Driscoll,' Sheena replied truthfully.

'Good,' he said. 'So we'll look for something a lot less defensive and a lot more co-operative, then, shall we? And now will you be kind enough to pour me another cup of this excellent tea?'

'Yes, of course, Doctor.' Sheena had been mentally preparing for a real blistering, and his firm but restrained reproof had wrong-footed her yet again. The only thing to do was to make no more mistakes—however trifling—and also to keep out of his way as much as possible. She was trying to frame an apology that would be neither provoking nor too abject when he asked suddenly, 'Why Craigstoun, Miss Scott?'

It was the sort of question bosses always asked sooner or later, but she hadn't expected it just at this point. Her main reason had been its nearness to David's isolated cottage in the hills, but she wasn't going to tell him that. 'You belong here perhaps,' he prompted.

'No, I'm from the west originally. I—I guess I just liked the idea of working in a centre such as this. Not many paediatric units have one.'

'I see,' he said, though she could tell he didn't

entirely accept her answer. 'You don't find the place somewhat lacking in its leisure facilities?'

That at least was easy. 'I don't have that much leisure, one way and another,' she admitted, allowing herself a brief smile. 'Dr Ferguson used to say that the best thing about Craigstoun was its proximity to Glasgow and Edinburgh.'

'The townsfolk obviously agree with him there. When I drove down the High Street last evening at nine it was practically deserted.'

'It's a different story at the bus station when the last buses get in.'

'Which further supports my predecessor's theory.' Another neat reminder that these were changed days and Matt Driscoll now occupied the director's chair!

'Quite so, sir.' Sheena was wondering whether she ought to make a move, or wait to be dismissed. 'Was there anything else, Doctor?' she asked as a feeler.

'A lot, as it happens, Miss Scott. Firstly I'd like to know which type of cerebral palsy you find hardest to treat.'

What a question! 'A child with little or no potential, I suppose,' she said slowly after some thought. 'It's so difficult to find the appropriate things to say to its anxious parents.'

'I wouldn't quarrel with that, but that wasn't quite what I meant. Surely there is one area of handicap with which you feel least able to cope?'

Was he looking for an expression of overall difficulty, or probing for specific gaps in her knowledge? She must be careful not to tie herself in knots. 'I think—I think the saddest cases are those where a child of above-average intellect has serious physical disabilities which prevent him reaching his full potential,' Sheena offered carefully.

Matt Driscoll picked up a biro and wrote a few words on his desk pad. Sheena would have given a lot to be able to decipher them. 'That is more or less a re-run of your previous answer,' he said then. 'Either you are deliberately misreading me in order to cover up——' he meant inadequacies for sure! '—or else your communication skills are indeed seriously flawed.' He paused to let that sink in. 'Time will tell, but for the moment I doubt that there is anything to be gained by continuing this discussion. Thank you for the tea, Miss Scott, but please don't feel obliged to make it every day.'

Don't worry, she was raging inwardly with frustration—I'll damn well let you dehydrate first! She stood up. 'I'm not very good at condensing my views on so vast a subject, Dr Driscoll,' she told him stiffly, 'but I've just completed a chapter on therapy for the updating of a textbook. I'll leave it on your desk tomorrow—and hope it can relieve your doubts.' And with that she marched out, pleased with her exit line.

However much Dr Ferguson and Beth Merryman's father had praised her, it was obvious that Matt Driscoll had serious doubts about her skill. At this rate she might be glad to look seriously at Mike's offer to help her to that job in Perth!

CHAPTER FOUR

'Oh, Sheena!' The YTS girl was looking horrified. 'Sharon and that dear little fair-haired boy have shut themselves in the Wendy house. Whatever shall I do?'

'Give me a minute and I'll show you.' Sheena settled Nancy safely in a chair in front of the big mirror and gave her a hairbrush. 'That'll keep her happy for as long as it takes,' she said. 'Now, you grab that side. The roof lifts off. See?'

'I should have realised that.'

'Not at all, lassie.' Sheena put on a playful scowl as she peered in. 'Now then, you two—out this minute or you'll get no pudding, and it's jelly with ice-cream today.'

'Dirty old woman,' snarled Sharon, resorting to her favourite insult.

'Look who's talking; you're chalk all over from head to foot.' Sheena unhooked the front and pulled it forward, removing their last defence against authority. 'If you're not out of there in one second. . .'

'Thanks so much,' breathed the girl. 'I was terrified that Dr Driscoll would come in.'

Sheena compressed her lips. Barely a month in the place, yet Dr Ferguson's successor seemed to have them all running scared. 'Where's Nurse Ramsay? I thought she was in charge of this wee group.' She'd have been for it had the director appeared.

'She is, but she's got this terrible headache and she asked me to keep an eye on them while she went for an aspirin.'

As she returned to Nancy Sheena made a mental note to have a word about the unwisdom of leaving somebody unqualified in charge. 'Now then, honey,' she said to her small patient, 'let's see if you can tie this nice ribbon in your hair. That's it—feet apart—steady now. Arms up. . .slowly. . .' How vital it was to turn all the necessary exercises into play or meaningful activity. Given luck and a lot of ingenuity, the children didn't realise they were being led into moving in the right way which they found so difficult. This was the first time Nancy had managed to stand for so long without grabbing the nearest hand-hold. Must remember to chart that before this afternoon. . .

'Sheena.' This time it was Jane interrupting. 'I'm very sorry, but I can't stay on for the case conference this afternoon. Nanny has just phoned to say that Baby is very fretful and is running a temp. I expect it's just her teeth, but I'm the only one who can comfort her when she's like this.'

Sheena sighed. 'Are you sure that the girl can't cope, Jane? Dr Driscoll will be very annoyed.' And add another black mark to their record sheet. 'You know he insists that we should personally present the reviews of our own patients' progress.'

'I also seem to remember hearing him insist that a mother is the right person to nurse her sick child,' retorted Jane.

'He was referring to our patients. I'm not sure he'd see staff problems in the same light.'

'Well, too bad,' said Jane. 'He can't have it both ways.'

Sheena admitted that Jane had a point, but it wasn't Jane who would be making it. 'All right, then—that's the way I'll try to put it to him. If I get the chance.' And then get a set-down afterwards for being cheeky, no doubt. Sheena sighed again. Work had always been so enjoyable before Dr Driscoll came.

She thought about that while helping to tie on bibs and generally get the children settled at tables for their lunch. Everybody was agreed that, professionally speaking, their new boss was a worthy successor to their beloved Dr Ferguson. His skill, knowledge and commitment were all much admired. But he continued to keep them all in the dark about his opinion of them. Obvious achievements were acknowledged, and deficiencies—of which he managed to find rather more—were pointed out with equal economy. His manner was always cool and correct. Everybody but Annie stood in awe of him, but then Annie could always change jobs any time and no bother, as she frequently pointed out. On balance, they were all secretly afraid that they weren't measuring up.

The weekly case conference was the only change Dr Driscoll had made so far to the centre's regime. It was his way of ensuring that everybody was kept in the picture. All senior staff had to attend, plus the physio and nursery nurse of the child under discussion. Parents too were asked, if appropriate.

A quiet word with Sister Charlie ensured that Betty's patients were first so that she could get away, and Jane's they kept until last to avoid provoking the director's displeasure early on, thus souring the whole afternoon. It worked. Dr Driscoll was actually smiling as he picked up Sayeed's notes and looked round for Jane. 'Will somebody fetch Mrs Clark, please?' he asked mildly.

'Er——' Sheena had to stop and cough to shift the slight obstruction that seemed to be hindering speech. 'I'm afraid that Mrs Clark had to leave, sir. Her baby is—very ill.' So much for that resolve to use his own argument against him!

Dr Driscoll was looking concerned. 'I'm very sorry to hear that. When was the child admitted?'

Sheena bit her lip. She might have known he'd think that after her dramatic way of explaining Jane's absence. 'She's—being looked after at home, sir.'

He frowned. 'I hope they're not taking any risks. What's the diagnosis?'

Tell him the baby is teething and then watch the roof fall in! We haven't heard, sir, but I gather the nanny was very—er—worried when she phoned.'

'I see,' A pause. Would he pursue it? 'Ah, well—it can't be helped—and presumably you know something about her patients, Miss Scott?'

'Oh, yes, sir,' sighed Sheena in relief before going on to paint a rosy picture of Sayeed's physical prowess. Then it was Moira's turn. She said that unfortunately his mental development wasn't quite keeping pace with his physical, and then his nursery nurse described him as a very happy little boy. The social worker said it was a loving, caring family and there were no problems at home. Finally Sister reported that he'd had no more asthma attacks. The rest of Jane's patients were as painlessly discussed and the meeting came to a close.

Dr Driscoll was the first to leave, and soon only Charlotte and Sheena remained to congratulate one another on getting through more or less unscathed. 'But you'd better give Jane a ring tonight—just to put her in the picture,' Charlotte advised as they left the room together.

Sheena promised that she would, but was forestalled by Jane herself, who phoned just as she was passing Reception. Annie had long since departed, so Sheena took the call. 'Her poor little gums are so swollen, the wee darling, and even ice doesn't seem to help,' reported Jane on hearing Sheena's voice. 'Neither of the others had half so much trouble; its wicked. One feels so helpless. Was Dr D very angry?'

'Not at all. He was very understanding, but——'

'I knew he would be,' interrupted Jane triumphantly.

'Only because I exaggerated,' returned Sheena, remembering to lower her voice as Dr Driscoll's room was only just down the corridor. 'But don't for heaven's sake let it out that the baby is only teething, or you'll land me right in it. I told him she was very ill.'

'OK, I'll remember that if he should ask me how she is. And thanks again, Sheena. You're a real pal.'

'Think nothing of it,' returned Sheena. 'See you tomorrow, then.' She replaced the receiver and continued on her way.

As she passed the director's room he appeared in the doorway. She hadn't heard him open the door, so it must have been ajar all the time she was talking to Jane. He confirmed as much by saying, 'I was listening out for you, Miss Scott. Can you spare me a few moments?'

'Yes, of course, sir.' She followed him in, heart thumping. Was it too much to hope that only her footsteps had been overheard?

'I've been asked to speak at a seminar arranged for this weekend by the local teachers of the handicapped, and I think it would be helpful if you could be there too,' he said.

Sheena breathed more easily. 'Of course, sir,' she said again.

One eyebrow rose ever so slightly. Had he expected her to hedge a bit? 'Fine, but I'd better tell you it's this coming Saturday evening.'

'Oh, dear—then I'm afraid I can't.'

'Because you have a date,' he assumed.

'Oh, no. Well, not exactly. I'm baby-sitting for little Dora Dewar. Her parents have been asked to a very special party, and as it's Saturday I doubt if anybody else on the staff will be able to stand in for me.'

The ghost of a smile flitted over Matt Driscoll's lean, chiselled features and was gone in an instant. 'Why not ask Mrs Clark?' he suggested in a velvety voice. 'After all, she owes you one after the spirited defence you concocted for her this afternoon.'

So he *had* heard! 'Oh,' breathed Sheena.

'Oh, indeed,' he agreed, folding his arms across his chest and continuing to regard her steadily.

'It's like this,' Sheena began, not at all sure what she would be saying next.

'Like what?' he asked when nothing else was forthcoming.

Sheena decided to pretend she hadn't guessed he'd overheard her chat with Jane. 'Mrs Clark isn't on the baby-sitting rota,' she explained truthfully. 'It is voluntary, and, with three wee children and a husband who is a busy GP, she simply doesn't have the time.'

'But I understood that she has a nanny.'

'So she has, but she's only part time.'

Matt Driscoll sat back on his desk, bringing himself down to Sheena's height. 'Do none of the married staff with children participate, then?'

'Yes, but the baby-sitting service is entirely voluntary,' Sheena re-stressed.

He didn't answer immediately. Then he said, 'Even though it is short notice, it is just possible that one of your volunteers may be able to change with you. But if not I think you should ask Mrs Clark. We'll call it a penance for taking this afternoon off for such a trivial reason, shall we?'

'I'm not sure. . .' faltered Sheena, meaning that she was doubtful of Jane's reaction.

'Then leave it to me,' he said calmly, surprising her further. She'd been expecting an explosion these ten minutes past—ever since she'd realised he knew she'd been covering up for Jane.

'Thank you very much indeed,' said Sheena with obvious relief.

This time there was no mistaking his smile as he commented, 'Just one of the penalties of being in the hot seat.' He stood up then and walked round the desk to take a sheaf of papers out of a drawer. 'I must apologise for not returning this sooner,' he said as Sheena recognised her chapter on therapy.

She took it, and because she simply had to know she asked, 'What did you think of it, Doctor?'

'I really don't think you could possibly have put things more clearly,' he answered.

'Oh, thank you, sir!' Sheena left the room feeling quite elated, but halfway to her office she paused. Had he meant that the subject couldn't have been dealt with more clearly—or just that she, personally, couldn't have managed to be more explicit? There was a world of difference between the two.

Saturday today, so the centre was closed. And as there were none of their small patients in the wards just now the day was all Sheena's until Dr Driscoll called to take her to his lecture. She hadn't expected him to do that— had told him she could easily drive herself there—but he had insisted. He said it was the least he could do when she was obliging him by going. Charlotte's right —he is mellowing, she thought as she switched on the washing-machine.

Comprising just the one decent-sized room, a bathroom the size of a handkerchief and a microscopic kitchen, Sheena's flat was hoovered and dusted by eleven. Then she went out to shop for the coming week before treating herself to a solitary pub lunch. She usually met Mike there for lunch on Saturdays, but this week he had cried off rather mysteriously. Sheena was inclined to believe that shaft about his having more than one pebble on his beach. Well, so have I, if I count David. Her face darkened as it always did when she thought of him. She had promised to go and see him tomorrow and she wasn't looking forward to it. One way and another, it looked like being some weekend!

Sheena spent the afternoon making notes for the evening. She hadn't been asked to speak formally, but Dr Driscoll had warned her that he meant to pass on all questions about physiotherapy to her. Numerous sessions with mothers' groups had taught her what to expect, but Sheena meant to have all the facts and figures on tap. She still hadn't decided which way to interpret Dr Driscoll's comments on her published work.

Mildly surprised, Sheena found herself taking longer than usual to decide what to wear. Why? This was a professional not a social occasion. Look neat and tidy, then, but not festive or even particularly fetching. She settled for a flared white skirt with a short, plain jacket of navy blue, worn with a white and navy spotted blouse. Her short russet hair always curled neatly round her small ears and a rare touch of eyeshadow added at the last minute gave an extra dimension to her dark-fringed, serious grey eyes. She put her purse, her notes and a few pamphlets in her briefcase, then remembered to look out a pair of gloves. I look quiet, efficient and completely unremarkable, she decided wryly after a final glance in her dressing-table mirror. The perfect sidekick, in fact. Would Dr Driscoll think so too?

Sheena appeared on the doorstep at the exact moment a dark grey Volvo stopped at the entrance. She had expected a white Ford and didn't recognise her boss until he leaned over and opened the passenger-door with a polite, 'Good evening, Miss Scott. You're very prompt.'

'Good evening, Dr Driscoll. And so are you,' she returned, getting in gracefully and fastening the seatbelt.

He gave her a brief appraising glance and directed a longer one at the façade of the building. 'Very well restored,' he observed judicially. 'I hope the interior is as good.'

'Yes, it is—I'm very pleased with my small corner of it.' Silence for a few minutes, and then, 'Have you managed to find suitable accommodation yet, Doctor?' Sheena asked politely.

'Not yet, but then there's no particular hurry,' he returned.

There wasn't much one could say to that without sounding curious, so Sheena merely remarked, 'How fortunate,' before commenting on the beauty of the evening.

'Yes—and it's much too good to be spent indoors,' he answered promptly. Sheena was wondering what he would rather be doing when he added, 'But I got in three sets of tennis between lunch and tea, so I can't complain.' He glanced sideways briefly. 'Do you play tennis, Miss Scott?'

She gave a deprecating little smile before admitting, 'I'm afraid I need a stationary target, so golf is my game.'

Matt Driscoll actually laughed at that. It was the first time Sheena had heard his laugh and she had to admit it was a very nice one. 'Are you telling me that golf is easier than tennis?' he asked incredulously.

'For me it certainly is.'

'So what's your handicap?'

'Fourteen,' she admitted ruefully. 'I can't get out on the course often enough these days.'

He actually whistled before saying, 'Don't be so modest, lassie. I know strong men who would give their back teeth for such a handicap.'

'Thereby ending up with another,' she riposted without thought.

'I'd no idea you were such a wit,' chuckled Dr Driscoll as he turned the car neatly into a side-street to avoid a snarl-up at the traffic lights ahead.

'You've soon learned your way about Craigstoun,' Sheena considered.

'Not really—this is my home town.' How come Annie had failed to unearth that titbit? 'Though we moved to Edinburgh when I was ten.' That must be how. 'And then my parents returned to their roots when my father retired last year.'

No wonder he didn't need to hurry his house-hunting. He must be staying with them. 'Most people do,' she observed, just for something to say.

That provoked another question. 'And where are your roots, Miss Scott?' Polite conversation or genuine interest?

'A tiny village in Argyll which hardly anybody has ever heard of.'

'That must be very peaceful.'

'Possibly, though I thought it deadly dull and I've not been back since my grandmother died. She brought me up after my parents were killed in a car crash.'

A sudden exclamation of shock or sympathy before Matt Driscoll said gently, 'My dear girl—I'm so sorry,' as he stopped the car in the forecourt of Craigstoun College of Further Education.

They found a packed lecture-room awaiting them. Whoever had organised the evening certainly knew all about publicity. A fussy little man in an old-fashioned suit came forward to greet them. 'So good of you to come, Dr Driscoll—and Mrs Driscoll too,' he presumed, causing Sheena to blush. 'How very nice.'

'Miss Scott is my senior physiotherapist and much more capable of answering any practical questions than I,' explained Matt Driscoll, seeming completely unruffled by the little man's *faux pas*.

Not so he. 'Dear me—so sorry—well, well. . .' babbled the poor man. 'So good of you to come, Miss Scott. So good. . .' He fussed them on to the platform, introduced them to the company, and the session began.

After a brief introductory talk by another speaker Matt rose to give his lecture. He pitched it at exactly the right level; neither too technical nor too trivial. He began with a simplified but clear description of cerebral palsy—the main reason for congenital physical handicap—and showed some excellent slides to illustrate the various types. Then he told how disabilities changed with each stage of the child's development and growth. 'But cerebral palsy is not the only congenital condition,' he said then, going on to outline various types of muscular dystrophy and others, such as Down's syndrome. In conclusion he said, 'We doctors are very good at telling parents what is wrong with their child, but very often it is the nurses, therapists, psychologists and teachers in special schools who modify and improve these conditions, thus helping the children to make the most of life.' He then sat down to warm applause, after which the chairman said that Dr Driscoll had kindly consented to answer questions.

As he had predicted, a lot of them were about treatment, and Sheena was frequently appealed to. She was nervous at first, but, being on familiar ground, she soon warmed up. Question-time lasted longer than Dr Driscoll's talk and Sheena was relieved when the chairman eventually called a halt and announced that coffee and sandwiches awaited in the refectory. It was now nearly nine and, having eaten nothing since lunch, she was feeling very hungry.

So she heard with dismay Matt Driscoll explaining that he had another pressing engagement and so, regretfully, they must be leaving.

The smell of freshly brewed coffee wafting up the stairs was too mouth-watering to be borne, so Sheena said as she was bustled out, 'I'll stay if you don't mind, Dr Driscoll. I can easily make my own way home——'

But by then he had her outside on the pavement. 'Don't be daft, girl,' he said. 'Have you not answered enough questions for one night?'

'I could bear a few more, especially as there's supper going with it. I'm awfully hungry,' she added wistfully.

'So am I,' he said, loosening his grip on her elbow to take out his car keys and unlock. 'But I've been to enough of these dos to know that question would follow question before you got anything more than halfway to your mouth. Get in.'

He drove several yards and then began to chuckle. 'I loved the way you fielded the questions about that place in Philadelphia. "The same techniques that we employ, but more intensively and to the point of exhaustion for all concerned, including the child",' he remembered. 'And then, "People always think that anything costing lots of money must be better than anything that's free." That was masterly. You're quite a student of human nature, are you not?'

'It helps,' returned Sheena abstractedly, while wondering how long it would be before her tummy started rumbling. 'But people will continue to take their children abroad to places like Philadelphia and Budapest until there are enough centres like ours to cope completely,' she rushed on loudly to drown the first undignified salvo.

'My goodness, you do feel strongly about that,' he remarked slyly.

He had heard, then—and, like the rest of him, his hearing was just too damned good. 'Well, of course,' Sheena returned strenuously. 'It's galling to read all this hype in the papers about places selling techniques we've known about and practised for years—and for free. Why can they not rave about the Bobath Centre in London? Everybody knows their methods are the most effective; they attract therapists and patients from all over the world. Why, when I was there——'

'Too near home and not pricey or fancy enough to be thought worthwhile,' he interrupted crisply. 'Besides, do you not realise that praising anything British is right out of fashion?'

All I know at this moment is that I am slowly starving to death, thought Sheena, sensing another volcanic rumble in the offing. 'If you were to turn left at the end of the Gallowgate and cut through the park you could get me home much quicker,' she told him. And what would be quicker when she got there? Omelette or scrambled egg?

'But I'm not taking you home,' he revealed at last. 'I owe you something after that magnificent show you put on tonight.' He parked his car outside Craigstoun's best Italian restaurant, and glorious visions of spaghetti smothered in some rich sauce floated before Sheena's eyes. She was out of the car before he could get round to open the door for her.

Sheena had been here several times with Mike and wasn't particularly put out when the proprietor greeted her by name and asked after 'Meester Macabetha'.

Once they were seated Matt Driscoll regarded her thoughtfully across the table. 'That man seems to be a bit of a gossip,' he observed. 'I hope he'll not be making any trouble for you.'

'Supposing he does tell Mike he's seen me? All I need to do is say that my boss kindly brought me here after we'd been working late.'

Matt grinned at her—suddenly and disturbingly. 'The idea is sound,' he allowed, 'but I'd phrase it differently if I were you. "I've been working late at the office, dear" is a well-known excuse that's worn a bit thin.'

Sheena giggled—it would have been impossible not to when he was looking at her like that—and Matt Driscoll said approvingly, 'That's much better. I'd begun to think you were altogether too dignified and serious to do anything so frivolous as to giggle.'

'But would you really like to be giggled at by your senior physio?' asked Sheena as the waiter handed them menus.

'Only when appropriate—such as now,' he told her firmly. 'What would you like to eat?'

'Spaghetti bolognese, please,' Sheena answered promptly.

'You're not afraid of putting on weight, then?' he queried after a swift but expert appraisal of what he could see of her.

'Not for the next decade or two at any rate. Besides, I'm famished.'

'So you said before. Right, then.' He turned to the waiter still hovering attentively. 'Spaghetti bolognese for us both, please—and you'd better make my friend's a double portion. Some mixed salad and a bottle of red Chianti, and after that we'll think again. All right?' he asked Sheena when the man had gone.

'Lovely, but I do hope he didn't take you seriously about that double portion.'

Another disturbing grin before he said, 'Don't worry, if he brings it and you can't cope I'll help you out. I'm fairly peckish myself after all that exercise this afternoon.'

'This is really extremely kind of you,' said Sheena next, on realising she hadn't yet thanked him for this unexpected treat.

'As I said, I owe you one.'

Which, of course, reminded her of what he'd said about Jane. 'You haven't told me who is doing my baby-sitting tonight, Dr Driscoll,' she reminded him.

'Haven't I? Well, it's Mrs Clark.'

'I say,' she breathed admiringly. 'I'd like to know how you managed that.'

'It was easy. I simply told her that she. . .owed us one,' they finished together.

When they stopped laughing, also in unison, Matt said thoughtfully, 'You know, you're really a very nice girl,' as if he had had serious doubts about that until then.

Sheena opened her grey eyes wide in reproach and said, 'I do try, so I'm glad it's showing.'

At that point the waiter returned with their food, and Matt kept his reply until the man had gone away again. 'As to that, don't we all? Try for approval, that is? Only it doesn't always work, does it?'

Sheena knew exactly what he meant. The staff at the centre still hadn't decided what to make of him—and he had sensed it. She leaned forward and said earnestly, 'Oh, yes, it does—given time. Truth will out, as they say.'

His expression was openly friendly as he responded, 'How very comforting, but all this philosophising is keeping you from your dinner. Do, please, begin.'

'Thank you.' Sheena picked up her fork, glad to see that the waiter hadn't taken seriously that order for a double portion. They didn't talk much while they ate, except to comment on the food, which was excellent. Then, as Sheena laid down her fork, Matt asked kindly, 'Feeling better now?'

'Much, much better, thank you. I could answer questions now all right—and no bother.' Earlier she had said 'I do like wine with my meals' and he had been unobtrusively topping up her glass ever since. The Chianti was good and it was potent.

'Careful,' he said, smiling. 'I might ask for your life story and, in your present expansive mood, you might tell it. Would you want to?'

'I've nothing to hide,' Sheena retorted, and that was absolutely true. On the other hand, she'd nothing particularly exciting to tell either. 'I've led a blameless existence,' she added.

'I find myself believing that,' said Matt, signalling for the waiter to bring them ices and coffee.

'Now you're gilding the lily,' said Sheena

'No—just storing up some goodwill, I hope.' He hesitated. 'Who knows? I might have another favour to ask of you some time.'

'Which I shall certainly comply with if I possibly can,' Sheena readily assured him

However, he didn't expand on that, just set himself to draw her out; getting her to talk about herself, her background, likes and dislikes. By the end of the meal Sheena felt he had nothing left to discover about her—except for the unhappy episode of David—while she knew next to nothing about him. So what? Theirs was a boss-and-subordinate relationship; nothing more.

When they got back to her flat Matt seemed in no hurry for Sheena to get out of the car, but kept her talking. Several of her neighbours had gone in with curious sidelong glances, and, rather than incur any more, she was just wondering whether to ask him in for a final coffee when he said abruptly, 'About that favour I mentioned earlier, Sheena.'

'Oh, yes,' she prompted encouragingly.

'Dr and Mrs Burnett are giving a party tomorrow night.'

Dr Burnett was the senior consultant physician on the hospital staff, and the party, she guessed, was to be a somewhat belated welcome for the newcomer. But Sheena couldn't quite see how she fitted in, though she learned next minute.

'The thing is, they've asked me to take a friend—if I wish—which, it so happens, I do. Only, being new to the town, I don't know anybody I could ask—except you. I really would be grateful if you'd come.'

He had surprised her—and very much. She simply couldn't see why he felt it so necessary to take somebody to a party where he would know at least half of the people present. Still, it was flattering to be thus singled out. 'You've got something else arranged,' he supposed when she didn't answer.

'Only a visit to a—a sick friend. And that doesn't

have to take all day. I'd like to go to that party—if it helps.'

'Bless you, I'm extremely grateful!' he exclaimed with a fervour that surprised her some more. 'It's to be drinks first and a buffet supper later, so would it be convenient if I picked you up about eight?'

'Fine. I'll look forward to it.'

'As I said before, Sheena, you're a very nice girl,' he told her with obvious sincerity as she got out of the car.

She watched until the Volvo was out of sight before climbing the stairs to her little flat. Why was Matt Driscoll so anxious not to go alone to the Burnetts' party? And why was it preferable to take one of the staff from his department when hospital staff were ever ready to detect the merest hint of gossip? Now that was an even more intriguing question!

CHAPTER FIVE

SUNDAY dawned fine and clear, and Sheena's first waking thoughts were for the new Matt Driscoll and the party they were going to that night. First, though, she had to visit David—a prospect that took some of the shine off the day. Sometimes she called herself a fool for putting up with him and his moods, yet it was difficult to cut loose entirely from somebody you had once thought you loved enough to marry—should he ask you. Especially when that somebody was at such a low ebb.

After breakfast Sheena packed a picnic basket. Even when David remembered to buy food it was seldom appetising.

He hadn't worked since being struck off the medical register some three years previously, and Sheena had no idea what he did for money; presumably he was living on Social Security. But, wherever the money came from, there was always enough to buy whisky, she reflected bitterly as she backed her little car out of the garage.

This fine May day had brought people out in droves, and the Criagstoun streets were busy. However, most of the cars were making for the Clyde coast resorts, and by the time Sheena headed into the hills there was not another car in sight.

David had chosen to hide himself away in a tumble-down cottage on a remote farm and, as always on the last lap, Sheena held her breath, half expecting a puncture as the car bounced and jiggled up the bumpy track. As she drew to a halt with relief David emerged from the cottage. She stared at him. Today his hair was cut and his beard was trimmed. He was also wearing new jeans and a clean shirt. Was he getting himself together at last?

The improvement extended to his temper. 'Nice to see you. Did you have a good journey?' he asked politely as she got out of the car.

'Yes—thank you,' she said dazedly. She'd been expecting abuse for being late.

'It's such a nice day that I thought we might go for a walk,' continued this resurgent David. 'But would you like a coffee first?'

'Yes—thank you,' she repeated, marvelling at the change. Has he won the pools? she was wondering as she followed him into the cottage. In the doorway she stopped and stared, because David's typewriter, long neglected, stood uncovered and clearly in use on the table.

He followed her glance. 'I've begun a novel—about a young hospital doctor wrongfully accused of causing a patient's death. Write about what you know, they say, and nobody can deny that I know all about that! You can read it if you like.' He went into the scullery and she heard him filling a kettle. By the time he came back with the coffee Sheena had read the first three pages.

'You've made a splendid start,' she enthused. 'I'd no idea you could write like this.'

'Neither had I,' he admitted. 'Could be I've found my true vocation at last.'

Only time would tell whether or not he was right; meanwhile the trying was obviously very therapeutic.

'How's your work going, then?' he surprised her

further by asking as they set out for their walk, taking with them the lunch she had prepared.

'Fine, thanks. Things were a bit dicey after Dr Ferguson retired—nobody knew quite what to make of his successor—but now we've got to know him better we really like him.' I do, at any rate, realised Sheena.

David stooped to pick up a pebble and throw it towards a crow perching on a fence. He missed it by a mile. 'Anybody I might know?' he asked carefully.

'I shouldn't think so. I'd never heard of him—he's not Glasgow-trained like us—and, anyway, he's only just got back from a lengthy spell abroad.'

'Doesn't seem likely, then,' he returned more easily. Recovering or not, Sheena guessed, he would always live in fear of his past catching up with him.

At the time of his trouble and disgrace Sheena had been at home in remotest Argyll, nursing her grandmother through her last illness. The authorities had managed to keep the affair out of the papers and she knew only those details which David had told her. Three long years it had taken for him to get over it. She prayed that his novel would succeed and complete the cure.

It was mid-afternoon when they returned to the cottage, where David had yet another surprise for Sheena. 'I don't know whether I told you that the farm has changed hands,' he began, looking slightly self-conscious. 'Anyway, the new people are being very decent to me about meals and so on. The thing is, I'm asked to high tea tonight, so I'll have to chase you off a bit sooner than usual. You'll come in for some tea first, though, I hope.' Once he would simply have told her it was time she went. And now she could stop worrying about telling him she was leaving early!

'Thanks—I'd love a cup,' returned Sheena, while

wishing she might have got a look at these benefactors of his. 'Are they a large family?' she asked.

'No—just parents, a son and a daughter.' He was looking self-conscious again, and Sheena thought she could guess why. It would do him the greatest good to acquire a girlfriend who knew nothing of his past—and it would also relieve her of this feeling of responsibility. Only now, when it looked like ending, could she fully admit what a very difficult time it had been.

'How long do you think it'll take you to finish the book?' asked Sheena when David had produced tea and a cake, courtesy of his new friends. Or, more specifically, their daughter?

But he couldn't tell her that. 'The first few chapters have written themselves; the difficult bit will be grafting on a happy ending.'

'You'll make it,' she said. 'I'm sure you will.' And she wasn't just referring to the book.

Sheena was halfway home before she realised this was the first time she'd ever visited David without his asking when she would be coming again.

She arrived home with two hours to fill before Matt Driscoll would be calling for her, and she spent them getting ready. A simple sheath of Thai silk in subtle blues and greens had hung undisturbed in her wardrobe since Beth Merryman's wedding. Now she took it out and pressed it carefully, thinking how well her new green sandals would suit it. Would Gran's pearls be going over the top? Remembering Mrs Burnett's consistently peacock-like appearance, no, it wouldn't.

Next Sheena took a leisurely bath with all the trimmings, then washed and blow-dried her hair. Careful make-up, and rosy varnish for her nails. It was ages since she'd taken quite so much trouble with her appearance. It was morale-boosting and it was fun.

It was also worth every second she had spent, judging by Matt Driscoll's reaction. He gazed at her as though he'd never seen her before. 'All I could have wished for,' he said slowly—and obscurely. Not quite the sort of comment she would have expected, but gratifying, still.

She rewarded him with a brilliant smile. 'Thank you, sir,' she said. 'I always try to please.'

'Then for heaven's sake don't ruin everything by calling me "sir" tonight,' he begged. 'The name is Matt, if you please.'

'I'll try to remember,' promised Sheena, while wondering how she could possibly spoil the party by not calling her boss by his Christian name.

Once in his car she watched him covertly as he moved round with easy grace to the driver's side. The slanting rays of the evening sun were striking unsuspected lights in his brown hair. She thought she had seldom seen such regular, yet completely masculine features in a man. And he certainly knew how to dress. His light fawn suit, pale buff shirt and Paisley-patterned tie were perfect for the occasion. No wonder old Mrs Grant, bottom left front, was curtain-twitching.

'I've no idea where the Burnetts live,' Sheena realised as they set off.

'About six miles out on the Stirling road, and I'm told I can't miss the house if I turn left at a pub called the Pheasant.'

'And it's such a gorgeous evening for a drive,' observed Sheena, settling more comfortably in her seat.

Matt glanced at her. 'All right? Because if not the seat is fully adjustable in all directions.'

'It's just fine as it is, thank you. This is a super car.'

'Isn't it? I only got it yesterday morning.'

'I'm awfully honoured to have been in on its maiden voyage.'

'And I'm equally honoured that you should have been.'

They couldn't possibly have kept up such extreme politeness, and there was silence for a bit until Matt asked, 'So how was your sick friend?'

'My——?'

'The sick friend you visited today.'

'Oh. . .much better, thanks, He really seems to be on the mend at last.'

'So he's been ill a long time, then?'

'Yes, years really. He had a nervous breakdown.'

'How very unfortunate.' He had sounded genuinely sympathetic, but Sheena doubted if Matt Driscoll had ever been in any danger of such an experience. His confidence came across as absolute. He, Sheena suspected, would be a rock in time of trouble. 'What was his job?' he asked suddenly.

No way would she reveal that David used to be a doctor.

'He's a writer—and rather a good one,' she returned, thinking of the extract she had read that afternoon.

'That explains it, then,' he considered. 'Artistic types are generally somewhat highly strung, are they not?'

Sheena couldn't think of a suitable reply, so she murmured something non-committal and remarked again on the beauty of the evening.

'What a blessing our weather is,' Matt observed wryly. 'When stuck for a subject we Scots can always fall back on that.' Had he guessed she'd only told him half the story? If so then Matt Driscoll wasn't exactly insensitive himself.

They reached the Burnetts' house not long after. It was a square sandstone Georgian gem, with a gravelled drive and perfectly manicured lawns all around it. Not at all unlike its mistress, decided Sheena as Matt backed his car skilfully into the last remaining space.

'The NHS cannot possibly be financing that all by itself,' he considered when he was able to take a proper look at the house.

'Rather not. Rumour has it that Mrs Burnett's father is a millionaire.'

'Lucky John Burnett,' said Matt. 'Remind me to ask him if his wife has a sister.'

'Have you met Constance Burnett?' asked Sheena as they strolled towards the house.

'Not yet. Why?'

'You'll know exactly what I mean when you have,' she returned demurely as they climbed the shallow steps to the front door.

'Ladies upstairs and first right—gents through yon door there,' said the gimlet-eyed housekeeper who met them in the hall. Sheena suspected that she severely disapproved of such frivolities as parties—especially on a Sunday.

'I'll wait here for you,' Matt promised as Sheena went obediently upstairs to leave her jacket. But when she came down again the hall was empty.

An excited buzz of voices wafted out through an open door to the right, so Sheena went to take a look. She found herself in a large double drawing-room full of people. At first she couldn't see Matt, then she spotted him at the other end of the room in a small group which contained the Burnetts and Poppy Menzies, the senior registrar in paediatrics. The likelihood of being able to fight her way through the crowd to reach Matt seemed wellnigh impossible, so Sheena got herself a gin and tonic from the bar close by and looked round for somebody to talk to.

She had reckoned without Matt Driscoll's resourcefulness, and barely a minute later he appeared beside her. She stared at him and asked, 'Now how in the world did you manage that?'

'Simple. When I saw you come in I escaped through the back window, round the side of the house, and in at the front door. Now we'll retrace my steps. Mrs Burnett insists that she's dying to meet you.'

A likely story, thought Sheena as he seized her hand in a strong warm grasp and towed her back the way he had come. By the time they arrived beside their hosts the Merrymans had joined the group. They promptly embraced and kissed Sheena, a display of affection which apparently impressed Mrs Burnett, who greeted Sheena rather more warmly than she had on the two previous occasions they had been introduced!

Meanwhile Poppy Menzies—tall, awkward, anxious and the wrong side of thirty—had lost no time in trying to wind herself once more round Matt. He forestalled her by linking a proprietary arm through Sheena's.

Mr Merryman being obviously ready with some saucy remark, Sheena was glad to see him seized upon by one of the hospital's general surgeons. Flora Merryman then forced Poppy into conversation, while Mrs Burnett proceeded to give Sheena the third degree. Dr Burnett had been ordered by his wife to circulate some minutes before.

'Phew! Now I see what you mean all right,' breathed Matt when hostessly duties finally obliged Constance Burnett to abandon the inquisition. 'But you were more than a match for her, Sheena. I loved the way you said so apologetically, "I'm afraid he was only a major", when she wanted to know your father's army rank.'

'Did you? I thought it was pretty awful of me—only

I couldn't resist it. She was patronising me so hard, and then I suddenly remembered hearing that Daddy, the millionaire scrap-dealer, had been a lance corporal in the army during the war. I'm not usually that bitchy,' she added, because it was beginning to be important that Matt should think well of her.

Judging by his expression, he was beginning to. 'I'm seeing a totally new Sheena tonight,' he said slowly. 'It could be something to do with that,' he said, pointing to her glass. 'Only it's empty, and as I don't want to lose sight of her we'd better go and get a refill.'

So back out through the french window they went and in at the front door to reach the bar. Then, spotting the senior nursing officer tacking determinedly towards them, Matt bundled Sheena out to the garden again. 'I had enough of her at dinner with the Fergusons last week,' he said firmly. 'The world is full of predatory females, Sheena.'

'And I know one or two men who are less than perfect,' she returned roundly, sending him off into chuckles again. 'I think I'm beginning to see why you asked me here tonight.'

'You don't know the half of it,' he sighed just as Poppy Menzies loomed palely into view by the light of the rising moon. 'Oh, my God,' he breathed. Then he snatched Sheena into his arms and kissed her.

He made an excellent job of it, and it was a good thing he had such a firm grip on her because Sheena's knees were right on course for collapse; something no kiss had ever done to her before. She was dimly aware of a stifled gasp and footsteps rapidly receding down the path.

To be on the safe side Matt gave it several seconds more before freeing Sheena. Then he said rather breathlessly, 'I suppose I should humbly beg your pardon.'

Indeed? It had been bad enough realising she'd only been asked along to play decoy duck, without that disturbing piece of window-dressing right on top of the discovery. Damn him! Had he no respect for her at all as a person? 'You may beg my pardon as much as you like,' she retorted furiously, 'but it'll not get you anywhere. How *dare* you use me so disgracefully? Next time you need a smokescreen I suggest you ring a call-girl agency!' And with that Sheena marched off towards the house, regardless of what the gravel was doing to her newest shoes. 'I'll bet that surprised him, the conceited bastard,' she muttered as she went. It was amazing what a spot of gin could do for a girl's courage and word power.

Once inside, Sheena went straight upstairs to repair the damage caused by Matt's surprising and expert attentions. She could apply lipstick, but there was no way of toning down the colour in her cheeks or the fire in her eyes. So what? This is an improvement, she decided. What price now the dedicated little mouse from the centre? Sheena knew just fine what most of the hospital staff thought of her.

It wasn't practical, though, to sit here admiring her reflection. Nor would it help anyone to have it suspected that she and Matt had fallen out. She would be pitied by the women and he would be angry—and ideally placed to retaliate at work, should any embarrassment result. She could guess it was Poppy Menzies she'd been dragged along to protect him from, so she'd already served her purpose. Right then. She'd not be actually seeking him out, but she would be charming and pleasant when they did meet. The homeward journey was going to be awkward, but there would be time enough to worry about that when the party was over.

When Sheena returned to the drawing-room Matt was talking to another paediatrician and his wife. He looked both animated and at ease—neither of which, she considered fiercely, he had any right to be. She turned away before their eyes could meet and went to get herself that drink she'd missed out on. As she took her first sip, up came the Merrymans. 'Well, well, well—and fancy seeing you here,' Beth's father began. Clearly he was about to indulge in some cumbersome teasing.

'You're no more surprised than I am,' Sheena told him swiftly. 'But it seems that Dr Driscoll was instructed to bring a girl, and as I was the only one in Craigstoun he felt he knew well enough he asked me. I had nothing better to do, so. . . Tell me, Mr M, dear, do you think that Canaletto over the fireplace could possibly be an original?'

Flora Merryman laughed delightedly. 'You're asking the wrong one, Sheena. He can't tell a Canaletto from a Christmas calendar.'

That earned her a wounded look from her husband before he returned to the attack. 'From what I've seen and heard, Matt knows Poppy Menzies quite as well as he knows you, Sheena.'

'So I gathered—tonight. Still, I can only tell you what he told me. He said I'd be doing him a favour by coming. And a girl, if she's smart, loses no chance of obliging the boss.'

Mr Merryman greeted that with a burst of rather ribald laughter. 'And a girl, if she's wise, also knows where to draw the line.'

'James, you're impossible,' his wife reproved him just as Matt came up to them.

'Was that a private joke, or can anybody share it?' he asked easily.

James Merryman took a deep breath prior to embarrassing Sheena some more, but she managed to get in first. 'Just my best friend's father taking advantage of my deplorable naïveté, but I'm well used to that. And not only from him,' she added significantly. Then she gestured with her glass to the painting over the fireplace. 'Perhaps you can tell us if that is an original, Dr Driscoll.'

A barely perceptible tightening of the mouth at the formality, but he turned obediently and looked. 'Difficult to tell at this distance, but I'd not be surprised. It would be entirely in keeping, would it not?'

Murmurs of assent from the Merrymans, and then the clanging of a gong brought a silence into which Mrs Burnett declaimed in her plummiest tones, 'Suppah is ready in the daning-room, everyone. Do *please* go and help yourselves.'

'Good idea; let's lead off, shall we?' suggested Beth's father, earning forgiveness. If the Merrymans were to stay with them Sheena would be very grateful.

But when they crossed the hall to join the queue—Mr Merryman hadn't been quite quick enough—Mrs Burnett pounced, saying, 'Now I really cannot allow you three to monopolise my guest of honour. Come along now, Matt, Miss Marchant is simply dying to talk to you.'

The senior nursing officer, whom he had successfully evaded earlier. 'Will you be needing your smokescreen, sir?' Sheena asked under cover of clanking crockery and cutlery.

Matt gave her an I'll-get-even-with-you-for-that look, while seizing her elbow in a vice-like grip and pushing her ahead of him.

'That's right, lad. Don't let her give you the slip,' advised James Merryman to Mrs Burnett's obvious displeasure. Clearly she thought that Matt Driscoll was wasted on a dim little nobody like his physiotherapist.

Fortified by her second gin and tonic, Sheena looked her hostess straight in the eye and said brightly, 'I believe your father was also in the army, Mrs Burnett, so that gives us something in common, does it not?'

At that Matt was obliged to suppress a chuckle, and the pressure on Sheena's elbow increased. Mrs Burnett merely grew an indignant inch or two and disdained to reply. Then, having delivered Matt to the SNO, she promptly departed.

'Of course, you will already have met my friend Sheena Scott, Miss Marchant,' Matt assumed tranquilly as he released Sheena at last.

'Oh—yes,' she returned doubtfully, which might have signified either yes to knowing Sheena, or doubt about his claim of friendship.

'Perhaps you're wanting to talk shop,' suggested Sheena helpfully. 'So don't worry about me, Matt, I'll just go and get myself something to eat.' Then she slipped away before he could stop her. An uncomfortable session with Miss Man-eater Marchant was only a fraction of his just deserts!

At the buffet, Sheena found herself beside Jock Stewart, Dr Burnett's registrar. He glanced at her incuriously, then did a double take at sight of her brilliant complexion, sparkling eyes and slim figure in her beautiful silk dress. 'Little Sheena Scott—is it really you? But you're looking fantastic.'

Rather a backhander, but still a compliment. 'It's so much easier to look decent when one is not hung about with small children,' she returned lightly. 'So what would you recommend out of this lot? It all looks so delicious.'

'The pâté's a dream, and the chicken mousse is good too. But how come you got invited? Old Mother Burnett's pretty choosy.' He reddened. 'Oh, God! Look, Sheena—I didn't mean——'

Sheena beamed on his discomfort and assured him she knew exactly what he had meant, lessening his embarrassment more than she could know. 'And I wasn't invited—at least, not directly. My new boss brought me along. I think he was feeling that some protection was required.' A quick glance across the table at Matt's scowling face assured her that he was still getting what he deserved.

Jock also looked and then chuckled. 'He'll not be too pleased with you for abandoning him, I'm thinking.'

'Oh, that's all right. He's over the worst now—and, as guest of honour, he's obliged to circulate.'

'Well, I'm not complaining,' said Jock, continuing to look at her as if he couldn't believe his eyes. 'Are you doing anything on Tuesday night?'

'Sorry,' she said, 'but my boyfriend is coming over from Perth on Tuesday.'

'Just my luck,' he said, 'but do you not think it might be more convenient to acquire one nearer home?'

'Distance no object, Jock. Mike has got a Merc.'

'Good lord, I couldn't compete with that,' he was saying, when Matt, having managed to shake off Miss Marchant, appeared beside them.

'Good of you to look after Sheena while I was busy, Stewart,' he said dismissively and, with a droll look for Sheena, Jock duly distanced himself.

'I don't think that was very polite,' she reproved.

'And you're an authority on politeness, are you?'

'More so than some folk I could name.'

'I can explain, Sheena. Look, let's go out to the garden——'

'No, thank you! For one thing, your choice of venue is very tactless and, for another, the Fergusons are heading this way.'

The four of them talked generally at first, but when Dr Ferguson started a discussion about the centre Sheena fell in with his wife's suggestion that they should go and sample the desserts. When Mrs Ferguson eventually fell prey to their hostess it was easy for Sheena to wander off and not rejoin Matt. She didn't expect him to seek her out again, but he did. Because Poppy Menzies is once more in evidence, she decided as he advanced on her purposefully with a cup of coffee in each hand. 'That was very brave of you,' she said, accepting one.

'To risk your righteous wrath?'

'To carry cups of coffee through that crowd. Somebody might have jogged your elbow and ruined that nice suit.'

'It's washable, but I'm so glad you like it. And my elbows are somewhat higher than average.' Which was very true. Matt Driscoll was six feet two if he was an inch, though with shoulders the width they were it wasn't that apparent.

'It must be wonderful to be able to look down on people,' suggested Sheena provocatively. Whatever had happened to that resolution to be pleasantly charming?

The look he bent on her then was frankly dangerous. 'Meaning?'

Sheena bore it with fortitude. 'Oh, just that I get very tired of being knee-high to a—a West Highland terrier.' She was five feet three.

'A very tall terrier for an equally tall story,' he contradicted flatly. 'There's not much that disconcerts you—as I am rapidly finding out. Unless, of course, it's just that you're drunk,' he said, walking away and leaving Sheena gasping with fury.

The party broke up around one and, for Sheena at least, that wasn't a moment too soon. She had got off to a good start with the chastening of Matt Driscoll, but had soon lost the initiative. And after that sparring over the coffee every round had gone to him. So it was ironic that, as they went upstairs to fetch their coats, Mrs Merryman should whisper to Sheena, 'I'm so glad you've found yourself a really nice man at last, dear.'

That was quite enough to make Sheena miss her footing and stumble up the last step. 'You've got it all wrong, Mrs M,' she insisted fervently. 'It really is just the way I told it.'

'Steady, now.' Mrs Merryman had grabbed Sheena's arm. Then she gave her a slow deliberate wink before assuring Sheena that her secret was safe with her. 'And I'll not mention it to Beth when I write—you'll want to tell her yourself.'

Sheena knew her friend's mother well enough to know that when Flora Merryman got an idea into her head nothing but a better one would drive it out. 'I do have a steady boyfriend, as it happens—his name is Mike Tennant and he's an insurance actuary. He drives a Mercedes,' she added, as if that could confer respectability.

'I have always maintained that insurance premiums are far higher than they need to be,' returned Mrs Merryman severely, disposing both of Mike and the whole insurance fraternity at one go. 'Now, then. When could you and Matt come to dinner?'

'I—don't know,' answered Sheena feebly. 'But how

is Beth?' she asked desperately on finding the bedroom full of other women collecting their things. 'I've not heard from her for weeks.'

Passing on the latest news of her beloved daughter was fortunately enough to distract Mrs Merryman until they were safely down in the hall again, where they found her husband and Matt putting in the time in earnest conversation. 'Talking shop,' she said with a certainty born of long experience. 'But one gets used to it.' She then advanced on Matt with a smile. 'I've been trying to get Sheena to name an evening when you could both come to dinner, but she's being very vague.'

Darling Mrs M, I could almost kill you, thought Sheena in acute embarrassment.

Matt flicked Sheena a look compounded of amusement and understanding. 'We'd love to come, of course, but could we take a rain check first?'

'Of course you can. Just give me a ring when you know. Sheena has our number.'

'We'll do that.' Matt took Sheena's arm, right under the nose of Poppy Menzies—who else?—and assisted her down the front steps of the house as if she were incapable of making it by herself. Oh, why did the Burnetts have to live way out in the country? In Craigstoun Sheena could have taken a taxi home—or even walked. As it was, she was facing the most awkward half-hour of her life. Well, almost.

The Merrymans had arrived before them, so their car was nearer the house. Having left them with renewed promises to be in touch, Sheena and Matt continued down the drive. 'All of that was quite unnecessary,' she said severely as soon as they were out of earshot. 'We both know perfectly well that we shall not be going to the Merrymans'—to dinner,' she added so that there was no mistaking her meaning.

'I'm very disappointed,' said Matt. 'I'm told that Flora Merryman is a wonderful cook.' After an infuriated hiss from Sheena he continued, 'I wonder if you're right, though? Perhaps it would have been better to say that you were merely acting as my minder tonight—and, as in the course of your duties you were forced to indulge in some repugnant practices, war has now broken out.'

Sheena could think of nothing to say to that. 'What's the matter?' he enquired. 'Did I not get it right? Is that not the way it is, then?' He unlocked the car and opened the door with a flourish.

'Nobody likes to be made fun of—or used,' said Sheena in a voice that throbbed with humiliation. 'You should have told me why you needed to bring me to this party, and if I had come—as I might have—anything that happened in the course of my duties, as you put it, would have been my own fault. As it is, the whole thing has been an insult. And if you can't see that then you're no gentleman!' She then collapsed, trembling, in her seat.

After a second's frozen silence Matt shut the car door and walked round to get in himself. They then drove off in continued silence.

Sheena was regretting her outburst quite bitterly. She had wanted to say something crushing, yet sophisticated and light, and the reason she hadn't managed it was becoming only too clear. She was seriously attracted to Matt Driscoll. But for that she could have regarded this whole evening as something of a joke—just as he did. But he attracted her, whereas to him she was just somebody who happened to be there and able to help him out of a jam. That's why she was so hurt and angry. Bad enough, but heaven only knew what damage that passionate outburst had done to her career.

Sheena settled her chin inside the turned-up collar of her jacket and stared miserably ahead, oblivious of the frequent sidelong glances coming her way throughout the journey.

She had taken out her keys and had her hand on the door-handle even before Matt stopped the car outside the flats. 'Goodnight,' she said stiffly and scrambled out.

Before she could open the outer door he was beside her, a hand grasping hers that held the keys. 'I told you I could explain and now I am going to,' he said softly but compellingly. 'Poppy Menzies has been making a nuisance of herself ever since I arrived. Her attentions are unwelcome, unsought and extremely embarrassing. So I got the idea that if I could show her I was involved with somebody else she would back off. So—yes, Sheena—I did use you and I'm heartily sorry for it.' He let go of her then, but only to transfer his hands to her shoulders. In the same quiet way he insisted, 'I kissed you in that garden to mislead Poppy. But this time it will be because I want to.' Then he drew her towards him and kissed her with a slow compulsion that touched her to the core. 'Goodnight, my dear girl,' he whispered. 'Please think over what I've told you and forgive me if you can.' Then he left her abruptly and went back to his car.

It was a very bewildered Sheena who climbed the stairs to home. Was Matt really beginning to take her seriously—or had he only intended to smooth her down?

CHAPTER SIX

SHEENA was still undecided when she awoke next morning. She wanted to believe that Matt was sincere, but common sense demanded that she should wait for further proof. She felt herself glowing afresh at the memory of that kiss in the garden. Was Matt Driscoll a self-centred opportunist—or was he not?

The slamming of a door and footsteps hurrying down the stairs alerted Sheena to time passing; normally she went out long before her neighbour in the morning. No second coffee, then; leave the dishes in the sink and dash. Even so, the first minibus-load of children got there before her. Suddenly she remembered that today was the first of Betty's week's leave with her husband. It was definitely going to be one of those days.

In the nursery Jane was already at work supervising the removal of the children's outdoor clothing. An aura of long-suffering resignation surrounded her, which sent Sheena's spirits down another notch. 'Gosh, I'm really sorry I was late,' she said before dropping down on her knees beside Tom, who, having taken off his anorak, was now trying to put it on again.

Once this little group was ready for their day, and with the next bus-load not here yet, Sheena seized the chance to placate Jane. 'How's wee Fiona today?' she asked. 'Are her teeth still bothering her?'

'You'd never believe the way that child is suffering. Graham had a terrible time with her when I had to go out on Saturday night. He hates being left alone with the children, even when they're well.' Jane took a deep breath. 'He says that if my work is going to disrupt our lives then I'll have to give it up.'

'Oh no!' The three of them could barely manage as it was, and if Jane left it would be a disaster. 'Jane, I promise you it'll never happen again,' Sheena assured her earnestly. 'It was a one-off—absolutely. But Dr Driscoll insisted that I should take part in the seminar and said that he personally would arrange for somebody to do my baby-sitting. And I did tell him you weren't on the rota. Anyway, never again. Promise.'

'Graham's going to phone him,' said Jane.

And I'd like to be a fly on the wall when he does, thought Sheena, but she merely said, 'That's probably best,' just as the second wave of children arrived.

Sharon was flushed and grizzling and her forehead was very hot to the touch. Hurriedly Sheena pulled off the child's coat and T-shirt to see her thin body covered with fiery red spots. Sharon had the measles. Promptly Sheena scooped her up and carried her to Charlie's room. They would isolate her, of course, but it was probably too late to avoid an epidemic. Immunisation was voluntary and only about half the children had been done.

Charlotte was furious with the nurse who had been on collection duty that morning. 'Why in the world did you bring this child in in this state?' she demanded.

'I had to, Sister,' said the girl, almost in tears. 'Mrs Lindsay has to go out, she said, so I had no choice.'

The gentle soul would be no match for Sharon's warrior mother and Charlotte knew it. She calmed down and said, 'All right, Nurse, put her to bed in the sick-room and remember to draw the curtains. See how the light is hurting her eyes? And then you'd better ring the hospital and tell Dr Driscoll's secretary.' Charlotte looked at Sheena. 'I shall have to examine

them all, of course, but I'll try not to get in your way—
I know Betty is on holiday.'

'All in the day's work, Charlie,' returned Sheena,
sounding more cheerful than she actually felt.

Today she started with Dinah, which provoked the
usual outcry. All the children wanted to be first, and
taking a different one every day for fairness cut no ice.
Childish memories were short. As usual, Dinah had
stiffened up over the weekend. Mothers were taught to
relax tight muscles, but not all of them acquired the
knack. 'Yes, I know, darling. You want to get your
gaiters on and stand up to look at the pictures, but
these naughty old legs'll not hold you up if we don't
sort your muscles first. . .'

All the other spastic children would be the same.
Betty called it the Monday Morning Syndrome. Must
remember to bring it into this afternoon's talk to the
mother's group. . .

Angus Duff was tearful. Was he missing his bosom
chum Sharon, or had he caught the measles too?
Sheena pulled up his shirt; no spots yet. Angus roared
with fury at such a liberty and tugged his shirt down.
Using only one hand, of course. Like some adults with
strokes, these children were quite literally unaware of
their affected arm. . .

When she saw Matt come in with Charlotte Sheena
was treating Angus in front of the big mirror, so that
he could at least see all of himself. . .or could he? Must
do some visual acuity tests when she had time——

'Sharon's got the measles all right, Sheena,' Matt
said easily. 'So we thought we'd better take a look at
her boyfriend. Do you mind?'

'No, of course not, Doctor. Anyway, I've finished
his morning session.'

'I hope you've had measles yourself.'

'And mumps and chickenpox and German measles.'

'The perfect paediatric physio, then,' he teased, raising a bit of a flush on Sheena's pale cheeks. She was thinking that he had no business to be so much at ease while she was still in two minds about his motives.

'In that case,' she said, 'I'd better be getting on with my work, or I'll be losing the title.'

Yet, in spite of not wasting a minute, Sheena was well behind when the playthings were cleared away and the tables set for lunch. Just as well that none of their children was in the hospital just now. She'd need every second for therapy here today.

At half-past two Annie came into the nursery looking rather sheepish. 'I say, Sheena, I'm awful sorry, but there's a new outpatient for you. Don D's secretary said the parents could only come at this time, so I said OK—and then I forgot to tell you.'

Sheena suppressed a sigh. 'Not to worry, Annie. If this is really the only time that suits them it wouldn't have made any difference. Show them to my room, please, and tell them I'll come just as soon as I've finished this treatment.'

Before that, though, a phone call intervened, so fifteen minutes passed before Sheena was able to go to her room.

The father was seated at her desk and didn't get up when she entered; just looked pointedly at his watch. 'Our appointment was for two-thirty, Nurse, and I'm a very busy man,' he said testily.

'I'm sorry you've had to wait, Mr Gibson,' Sheena returned quietly, 'but, with one of my staff away, I'm very busy myself. Besides, I didn't know you were coming.' Sheena turned and smiled on the anxious mother and her baby. 'How old is wee Derek now?' she asked gently.

Before Mrs Gibson could open her mouth her husband jumped in with, 'We want Derek treated privately, Nurse.'

'We have no provision for that, Mr Gibson, nor do we consider it necessary. Every child here has a specially prepared programme tailored to his particular needs. And perhaps I should say that I am not a nurse—I am Miss Scott, the physiotherapist in charge. Now I think I should examine your son.'

The next hour was difficult, with Mrs Gibson trying to answer Sheena's questions while her husband demanded to be told the purpose of every test. Fortunately the baby seemed to enjoy all the movement and attention. He had had the triple immunisation, so there was no problem about starting treatment right away.

The Gibsons eventually departed reasonably satisfied, and as the nursery children too would have gone home by now Sheena headed for the kitchen to make herself a cup of tea.

'Sheena?' Matt had come to the door of his room. 'You look as though you had the weight of the world on those slim shoulders of yours.'

Was he really sympathetic, or was he merely trying some more buttering up? 'This measles outbreak is going to make things difficult,' she said. 'When there was an epidemic of chickenpox last year Dr Ferguson closed the nursery to the vulnerable children, so we treated them at home as often as we could. I don't need to tell you what that did to their timetable—and ours.'

'At the risk of being thought contrary, I propose to keep them all coming in. After all, the infection is spread before the spots come out, so the damage—if any—is already done. Does that relieve your mind?'

'Yes, thank you—up to a point. But what about the

ones who do catch measles? They're bound to slip back in their development.'

'Of course, but you can't do the impossible, Sheena, so I suggest you stop trying. What did you make of the Gibson boy?'

'To my mind he is the typical floppy baby, but I'll be interested to hear what Moira—Dr Cantlay—has to say. It seemed to me that the wee soul is none too bright.'

'You're right, but let's hope he's just a late developer.' He grinned at her in that way she was beginning to wish he wouldn't. She didn't want him to turn out to be one of those men who thought they only had to smile at a woman for her to do anything they asked. 'How about continuing this chat in my room over one of your special tea-trays?' he asked softly.

'Certainly I'll make you some tea, but I have to go and talk to the mothers' group very soon.'

The grin disappeared and Matt said quietly, 'In that case, I wouldn't dream of troubling you. I'm perfectly capable of making a pot of tea.'

Sheena watched him stride off to the kitchen. She'd snubbed him and he had minded. Was she wrong, then, to doubt his sincerity? If only she had more faith in herself, but five years of David's egotism and six months of Mike's casual take-me-or-leave-me approach had eaten away at a self-esteem which was never very secure in the first place.

As usual, it was Connie Burns who orchestrated the mothers' meeting. 'Did you find out any more about that self-catering holiday scheme, Sheena?' she asked as soon as Sheena opened the door.

'Yes, I did. They've sent me some leaflets and I got these copies run off.' She dumped them on the table. 'The chalets all have ramps to allow easy access for wheelchairs. Oh, yes—and they suggest that you get a letter from your GPs, listing any special problems, so as to put the local doctor in the picture should any child be taken ill. Now, then, have you all got your questions ready?'

They had, and there were more of them than usual, so Sheena could only briefly mention the question of trying to keep the children's muscles relaxed over the weekend. 'We'll go into this more fully next time,' she ended. 'Do you think your Bobby would mind helping us out, Connie? It's easier to get the message across if I can demonstrate.'

'You can count on it, hen. I never saw such a wean for showin' off.'

'Great. Well, if nobody else has any more queries. . .' Nobody had, so the meeting broke up.

'Are you seein' your fella the night?' wondered Connie aloud as she walked with Sheena as far as the exit.

'No, I'm sitting in for a new baby tonight. I don't think you've met her mother yet.' Sheena looked at her watch. 'And if I don't get my skates on they'll be standing in the road looking out for me.'

'Yours is less of a job and more a way o' life,' observed Connie shrewdly as they parted.

It was back to the flat for a shower and a complete change of clothes; Sheena never risked carrying infection to children in their homes. This left little time for a meal, so she made a sandwich, drank some orange juice and snatched an apple to eat in the car. She could always stop for a take-away on the way back—if she wasn't past it by then.

The minute Sheena saw the baby she knew that she was ailing. She was fretful, crying and restless. 'How long has Kelly been like this?' she asked.

'Since about lunchtime. My husband reckons it's her teeth.'

Sheena thought it might be more than that, but she didn't want to alarm Mrs Morrison. 'Did you not call your doctor?'

'I didn't like to—not just for teeth.'

'I see—well, have a nice evening, the two of you, and try not to worry,' Sheena added, though neither parent seemed inclined to. She had already decided to ring their GP as soon as they were out of the house.

But before she could do that the baby had a fit. Having dealt with that, Sheena took her temperature and found to her horror that it was almost forty degrees centigrade. There was only one thing to do and Sheena did it. She wrapped the child up and put her in her carry-cot. Then, with the cot wedged firmly on the back seat of her car, Sheena drove post-haste to the hospital.

The charge nurse on duty in Accident and Emergency took one look at the child, who was now frankly drowsy, and said, 'It was a good thing you were there, Sheena,' before putting out an urgent call for Poppy Menzies.

They had made it a rule that parents availing themselves of the baby-sitting service should always leave a number where they could be reached, so when Poppy appeared Sheena melted away to phone the Morrisons. Then she went for a walk round the hospital grounds. No way could she have gone home without hearing the verdict.

'Meningitis,' said the charge nurse when Sheena returned to A and E. 'Viral, we assume, but we'll not know for sure until the lab reports are back.' He chuckled. 'Dr Driscoll was full of praise for your

Take 4 Medical Romances

Mills & Boon Medical Romances capture all the excitement and emotion of a busy medical world... A world, however, where love and romance are never far away.

We will send you **4 MEDICAL ROMANCES** absolutely FREE plus a cuddly teddy bear and a mystery gift, as your introduction to this superb series.

At the same time we'll reserve a subscription for you to our Reader Service.

Every month you could receive the **4** latest Medical Romances delivered direct to your door postage and packing FREE, plus a free Newsletter filled with competitions, author news and much more.

And remember there's no obligation, you may cancel or suspend your subscription at any time. So you've nothing to lose and a world of romance to gain!

FREE

FILL IN THE FREE BOOKS COUPON OVERLEAF

Your Free Gifts!

Return this card, and we'll send you a lovely little soft brown bear together with a mystery gift.... So don't delay!

FREE BOOKS COUPON

YES Please send me 4 FREE Medical Romances together with my teddy bear and mystery gift. Please also reserve a special Reader Service subscription for me. If I decide to subscribe, I will receive 4 brand new books for just £6.40 each month, postage and packing free. If, however, I decide not to subscribe, I shall write to you within 10 days. The free books and gifts will be mine to keep in anycase. I understand that I am under no obligation - I may cancel or suspend my subscription at any time simply by writing to you. I am over 18 years of age.

EXTRA BONUS

We all love surprises, so as well as the FREE books and Teddy, here's an intriguing mystery gift especially for you. No clues - send off today!

1A2D

Name (Ms/Mrs/Miss/Mr) _____

Address _____

_____

Postcode _____ Signature _____

Reader Service
FREEPOST
P.O. Box 236
Croydon
CR9 9EL

SEND NO MONEY NOW

NO
STAMP
NEEDED

initiative, which didn't go down too well with Dr Menzies.'

That figured, but Sheena wasn't too interested in Poppy's reaction. 'Dr Driscoll?' she repeated. 'How did he get in on the act?'

'He's the paediatrician on call tonight. Your precious little centre isn't his only responsibility, you know.'

'I do know—and dinnae you be sae cheeky, Ned Buchan,' returned Sheena, rising as expected to the provocation. 'Did the baby's parents turn up?'

'Hotfoot in response to your message. They're with her up in Isolation now.'

'That's all right, then.' Sheena stifled a yawn. 'I only wanted to make sure I'd not pressed the panic button unnecessarily, so I'll be getting home now—it's been a long day.'

'You do that, Sheena. The Morrisons did say they hoped to see you to thank you, but that can wait until tomorrow.'

'In that case. . .' Sheena didn't go home after all. The Morrisons had said they wanted to see her, and right now they needed all the support they could get. She left her car where it was and crossed the grassy quadrangle to the paediatric block. As she mounted the steps Matt Driscoll came out.

He stared at her. 'And where are you going?' he asked. Not sternly exactly, but he wasn't smiling either.

Sheena blinked. 'I was going to have a word with baby Kelly's parents. Charge Nurse Buchan said they were asking for me.'

'I'd have thought you'd done enough for them for one day.' Matt's keen eyes searched her face. 'You look tired, Sheena, so why not just go home?'

'I'm not really. How's Kelly now?'

'Very ill, but stable. It would have been a different

story, though, had you not been there to act so promptly. Well done. . .' He didn't need to continue.

'But if she recovers she'll be even more handicapped than before,' Sheena supposed bleakly. 'And as her prognosis was no poor anyway. . .' Now it was her turn to leave the unsayable unsaid.

'You did the right thing, Sheena.' Matt was quite positive about that. 'The rules are quite clear for everybody but us poor medics. We're the ones who are occasionally called upon to play God,' he added heavily.

'That's why I finally decided against medicine. I don't think I could have coped with that.'

'I sense a story in there somewhere,' said Matt in something more like his usual manner. 'I suppose. . .' He paused. 'If you're really not too tired I suppose you wouldn't care to tell it over a plate of something at the hotel round the corner?'

'Not really—it's not worth telling,' said Sheena, cheered to see a flash of disappointment he didn't quite manage to conceal. 'But the food bit definitely appeals. I hadn't time for more than a snack before going to the Morrisons'.'

'Then what are we waiting for?' he wondered. 'Do you mind walking? It's no distance, going out by the side-gate.'

'Does this mean that I'm forgiven?' Matt asked carefully as they set off across the grass.

'It means that I'm giving the matter my earnest consideration,' was as far as Sheena would go.

'I'm in your hands,' said Matt with exaggerated humility. 'Oh, blast! The gate is locked.'

'But it's quite easy to climb over it.'

'Sheena Scott, you shock me! I'd never have suspected you of anything so irregular.'

'I can be as irregular as anybody else when it's called for,' she retorted.

'Not exactly a matter for pride, I'd have thought. Still, you've obviously done this before, so what's your method?'

'Inelegant, but functional,' returned Sheena, placing one foot on the centre cross-bar and hauling herself up by her hands. Then she swung first one leg and then the other over the top and dropped down on to the pavement.

'I see what you mean,' said Matt unflatteringly. 'Now, then, stand clear if you value your life.' He took a run at the gate, grabbed the top of it with one hand and vaulted over with the ease and grace of a panther.

'Long legs confer an unfair advantage,' said Sheena as he dusted off his hands before taking her arm.

'There's no need to be so crushing—just because you're only knee-high to a Westie,' Matt retorted slyly.

She recalled with startling clarity how furious she had been with him when she had said that. But she wasn't angry now—far from it. Besides, she'd read somewhere that it was a sign of interest when a man remembered all the silly little things a girl said to him.

They were nearly at the hotel now, and as they waited to cross the road two of the junior doctors emerged. 'This place is within bleeping distance, so it's very popular with the hospital staff,' warned Sheena.

'So how do you suppose I got to hear about it?' Matt asked tranquilly.

'Just thought I ought to mention it.'

He steered her over the busy street, giving the two young doctors a cheery greeting in passing. 'Why?' he asked then.

'Well, somebody might see us together, I thought. And so they have.'

'Have you got something to hide?' he asked next.

'Certainly not!' Sheena was indignant.

'Well, neither have I. In fact, as you know very well,' he continued silkily, 'I have every reason to want to be seen about with an attractive young lady.'

'As long as it is only a matter of *being seen*,' stressed Sheena, 'then I don't mind helping out.'

'Don't worry—I'm not much given to sudden embraces while eating,' he reassured her as they entered the dining-room. 'The sheer physical difficulties are too much to handle.' He looked round the room, which was almost empty. 'Is this place really as good as it's supposed to be?'

'Oh, yes, it's excellent, but you get the same food cheaper in the bar across the hall.'

'No, thank you. Eating off tables eighteen inches high is extremely uncomfortable when you're built like a beanpole.' A reproachful look went with that remark.

'Did I really say that?' asked Sheena with pretended remorse.

'Not directly. You were a little more subtle.'

'Thank goodness for that. On the other hand, if you want to be seen wouldn't the bar be better?'

For answer Matt pulled out a chair from the nearest table and placed her in it, gently but firmly. 'Much more shilly-shallying and the place'll be closing for the night,' he said. Then he rang the bell for the waiter.

They ate steak, salad and cheese, while continuing to spar verbally between mouthfuls. When the waiter brought the coffee Matt reminded Sheena what she'd said earlier about not studying medicine.

'My grandmother suggested it when I said I wanted to work in a hospital. Her point was that I'd be quite alone in the world when she was gone and, as she hadn't got much to leave me, I'd have to provide for myself. So she reckoned I'd better choose a reasonably well-paid profession.'

'Prudent perhaps, but not very flattering.' Sheena looked a question and he added, 'Did she not expect you to marry?'

'I've no idea,' Sheena returned honestly. 'Anyway, that's not something to bank on these days. Not when so many people don't bother—or else get divorced if they do.'

'You don't take a very rosy view of life, do you?'

'I've no particular reason to,' Sheena admitted.

'Some man has hurt you very badly,' guessed Matt, sounding almost angry.

'Not really—not in the way you mean. I guess it's just that I'm the sort of girl men find—find. . . If I knew the answer I'd be able to get myself sorted out,' Sheena finished gamely. She had almost said 'find useful rather than madly desirable', but there was no need to put oneself down that much. Besides, Matt would have taken that personally and that would have been a pity when he was being so nice to her now.

'Not knowing the answers is the reason we all make mistakes,' he offered gently. 'Personal relationships are the most important things in life. Yet how many of us get them right?'

So he too had had his troubles. 'Yes—as little Bobby Burns's mother would say, life's a right bugger. She lurches from one disastrous relationship to another, and yet she's one of the most cheerful people I know. Could be that's the answer, then.' Sheena giggled, largely from relief at having got the conversation on to a lighter plane. 'Connie's always wanting me to go with her to some disco or other. Perhaps I should take her up on that.'

'I don't recommend it,' said Matt. 'Apart from anything else, you'd probably end up deaf, and that'd be a tremendous handicap in your job.' He grinned at her and this time the grin was reassuring.

By now they were the only people left in the dining-room, and the ostentatious way the waiter was clearing tables prompted Matt to say with a sigh, 'Perhaps we'd better be making tracks before he throws us out with all the other debris.'

He paid the bill and they strolled back to the hospital; the long way round this time. Matt had said firmly that he never vaulted over gates after meals, while Sheena found herself hoping that it was really because he wanted to extend this time together. The talk was light and easy and they laughed a lot—and they reached the main gates just in time to see Poppy Menzies driving out. She saw them too, or why else would she have swerved like that on an empty road?

'Sometimes I worry about Poppy,' admitted Matt, staring thoughtfully after her rapidly receding car.

Oh, he did, did he? 'Then why did you go out of your way to—to distress her at the Burnetts' party?' wondered Sheena somewhat tartly.

'Good question.' He hesitated. 'But then, I didn't fully explain the situation, did I?'

'You said enough.'

'For then perhaps, but now I want to tell you the whole of it.' He waited a few seconds, marshalling his thoughts, and then began, 'Poppy and I go back a very long way: we were in the same year at medical school. Half a dozen of us got into the habit of going round together, and it was some time before it dawned on me that everybody thought of Poppy as my girl. When it did it didn't bother me too much. There wasn't anybody else I particularly fancied, and Poppy was—all right. She was good-natured, helpful—always offering to cook meals for me and do my washing. I'm sure you know the sort of thing I mean,' Indeed she did. There was a close parallel there to her relationship with David.

'The trouble began in our first clinical year when I started dating a pretty student nurse. Poppy carried on then like a wronged wife of thirty years' standing. I finally managed to make her face up to how things really were between us, and afterwards we went back to being good friends again—or so I thought. Eventually we graduated and went our separate ways, but soon Poppy turned up again, and to cut a long story short, Poppy was the main reason I went abroad two years ago. I have to admit I'd almost forgotten her until I came here, and there she was—the same old Poppy, only twice as determined. Cold-shouldering has no effect at all and, quite frankly, I'm at my wits' end,' Matt wound up on a heavy sigh.

It was on the tip of Sheena's tongue to suggest he got married, or went abroad again, until she realised just how little she would like him to do either! So she said, 'I'm so glad you told me— it makes everything quite understandable now. And if I can help out again some time don't hesitate to ask.'

'That's very generous of you, Sheena,' Matt said warmly. 'Look, I'm off tomorrow evening, so how about helping me to lay another smokescreen then?'

'Sorry, but I can't. My friend is coming over from Perth.'

'Too bad,' he said, actually looking quite disappointed. 'Still, at least I can drive you home tonight.'

By then they had reached her car, parked in the

forecourt of A and E. 'That's very kind, but this elderly heap here belongs to me.' If only it hadn't been in full view she might well have been tempted to accept his offer.

'Looks as if this is it for now, then, but I shall hold you to your offer.' Then he bent down and kissed her, even though Poppy Menzies must have been streets away by now. 'Thank you for this brief interlude, Sheena,' he said quietly. 'I've really enjoyed it. Until tomorrow, then.'

As she drove away Sheena looked in her rear-view mirror. She saw Matt put a thumb on the communicator in his top pocket before hurrying into the building. Another emergency call. He wouldn't have been able to take her home anyway.

CHAPTER SEVEN

MIKE hated to be kept waiting, so Sheena was ready in good time. Then he himself was late, but Sheena knew better than to remark on that when he did appear. She put in the time going over her day.

Besides Sharon, three other children were off with measles. There had been no crises and very few tantrums among the rest. So it should have been a joyride, and it hadn't been. Sheena had enough self-knowledge to realise that was because she hadn't clapped eyes on Matt; at least, not to any purpose. All she'd seen was his back view as he'd disappeared into his room at half-past two. Knowing the exact time was a bad sign. She was getting far too interested in the man before she had definitely established that the interest was mutual and sincere. It was quite a relief when Mike eventually hammered on the door.

He didn't apologise for being late—that wasn't his way—just fumed about being overworked and then about all the traffic on the roads. 'It would have been a damn sight more convenient if you had taken that job,' he ended as they drove off.

It's almost as though he classes me as just another annoyance, thought Sheena wryly. 'Why do we not take it in turns, then?' she asked. 'I could always come through to Perth alternate weeks.' Their meetings had dwindled to once-weekly affairs. 'Did you have anything particular in mind for tonight?' she asked next, never dreaming what might be coming.

It was over coffee after spaghetti at Giovanni's that

Mike dropped his bombshell, though he led up to it with some attempt at finesse. 'Do you see us going anywhere?' he began idly.

Sheena didn't immediately catch his meaning. 'I'm not sure I follow you,' she said.

'We've known each other nearly six months now.'

'Yes, it must be about that.'

'And never before have I been out this long with a girl without going to bed with her.'

'I see,' said Sheena, though she didn't really. Apart from the odd kiss, Mike had never shown that much interest in her. Until, that was, his suggestion for moving in if she took that Perth job. 'So you think you're wasting your time,' she assumed.

'Well, so I am—aren't I?'

'You obviously think so.'

'That's why I'm thinking of asking Janice at the office if she'd like to move in with me. You had your chance,' he added.

'So it seems—and I never took it. The story of my life.'

'It's not too late,' he added magnanimously.

My God, she thought. He simply doesn't have a clue! 'That's most generous of you,' she returned, tongue in cheek. 'But, since Janice obviously suits you——'

'I'd rather have you,' he said belatedly.

Is he mad? Sheena wondered, dazed. Had he really thought to bring her to the boil, so to speak, by threatening her with this Janice? It wasn't exactly an unknown ruse, but surely never before tried quite so clumsily. 'We've been at cross-purposes all along, I guess,' was the best she could come up with.

'It's this way you have of seeming so detached that

got me interested,' he revealed. 'I'm not used to it. It was a challenge.'

For a fleeting moment Sheena wondered if things might have turned out differently if they'd talked this frankly from the beginning. Probably not. . . Impatiently she thrust aside the sudden intrusion in her mind's eye of Matt's lean, humorous face. 'Look, Mike,' she said, 'I've enjoyed our times together and I'm really sorry to have disappointed you. But things seem to be turning out all right for you. I hope you and Janice will be very happy.'

He looked quite alarmed at that. 'Look here, we're not getting married!'

'I gathered that.' But surely he expected they would be happy, or else why was he moving her in? Did he just see the poor girl as one more handy domestic gadget? Charming! 'But I'm still hoping that you'll be happy.'

'So am I,' he returned, though without much conviction.

Mike drove Sheena back to her flat, but when she asked him in for one last coffee he refused, saying there didn't seem much point. The end of an imperfect friendship, she thought philosophically as she watched him drive away.

Next day two more children were off with measles, making six altogether. 'A pity for them, of course,' allowed Jane, 'but what a blessing it happened while Betty is off. Otherwise we'd have been completely snowed under.'

'How practical you are,' Sheena observed gravely on hearing that. She turned to Bobby. 'Now, then, m'lad, did your mum tell you I need your help on Friday?'

'Aye—an' I'm yer man any time.'

'You're a pal, Bobby. I knew I could count on you.'

'It'll cost ye, mind. I'm wantin' a go on the climbing frame.'

'Oh, lovey—I'm not sure you're ready for that yet.'

Bobby put on a mulish expression and Sheena relented. 'All right, but the minute you start to stiffen up then off you come.'

But he managed better than she'd thought he would, and then Nancy demanded to have a go. A different matter, this, with her general unsteadiness and difficulty holding on tight enough. Still, she'd have to progress from being helped sooner or later. It was a rather hair-raising experience, though, and Sheena was glad when the mid-morning milk and biscuits were brought round, putting an end to it. Nancy loved her food almost as much as she loved her own reflection.

There was quite a crowd gathered around Annie in the kichen when Sheena went to make herself a coffee. 'I couldn't decide which one was actually with him,' Annie was saying, 'but they both looked as if they'd like to be. But then, the other guy was pretty gruesome. Too fat, red in the face and constantly coughing.'

'One blonde, one dark, and both gorgeous,' recapped psychologist Moira. 'I wonder who they are? You're quite sure you didn't recognise them, Annie?'

'Positive. They're definitely not on the staff here.'

'So what have I missed then?' Sheena asked curiously when she could get a word in.

'Annie saw Dr D in a foursome at the MacRobert Theatre in Stirling last night,' explained one of the nurses.

Did she indeed? So much for that touching little cameo of himself at home with only a book for company! 'What was the play?' asked Sheena, as if that were the most important bit as far as she was concerned.

'Not a play—a concert. A lot of dreary old classical stuff—and we only went because Bob's boss gave us the tickets when he couldn't use them himself.'

So Matt Driscoll liked classical music. Unless, of course, he'd only gone along for the company. He certainly had a better evening than I did, thought Sheena as she gulped down her coffee and hurried back to the nursery.

Having revealed all, Annie was now back at her desk, and she caught Sheena in passing. 'Phone for you, Sheena. The Don,' she added without covering the mouthpiece.

'Good morning, Dr Driscoll,' said Sheena primly.

'You sound quite terrifying,' he riposted humorously. 'Have you had some bad news?'

That depended entirely on how you looked at things! 'Just being polite, sir. What can I do for you?'

'Sound a bit more friendly, for a start,' he said. 'But seriously. I've just seen wee Kelly. She's responding fairly well to treatment, but the reflex contractions are stronger than ever, so she's needing your attention. Can you fit her in?'

'Of course, Doctor. Would this afternoon be soon enough?'

'Surely—I know that's when you like to treat your ward patients.' There was a murmured interruption at the other end of the line and then Matt said, 'Sheena?'

'I'm still here.'

'Good. So what time will you be over?'

'I've been reconsidering. Kelly is very difficult to position, so I think I'd better make it before lunch.'

'Splendid! Then I'll probably still be here,' he said enthusiastically before ringing off. Because he knew that Poppy would also be there to get an eyeful? Well, you did offer to help, didn't you—you mug? What's the matter with me, as if I didn't know. . .?

Jane was looking quite distracted when Sheena returned to the nursery. 'Dinah's just tipped all her finger-paints over Sayeed and he's furious,' she said.

'I'm not surprised; I'd be too. Where is he?'

'Nurse Carter's giving him a bath—it was the only thing. And I say, Sheena, what d'you make of this? I've got wee Simon down as a spastic diplegia, but if those writhing movements he's started making are not a sign of athetosis then I'm a go-go dancer. . .'

'Dr Ferguson's first rule: never pin labels on a very young child,' Sheena reminded her. 'Because they change and evolve as they develop. Let's see now.' She peered into the cot. 'By golly, you're right, Jane. Better bring this to Dr Driscoll's attention.'

'You do it, Sheena. I'm not talking to him—remember? Will this make any difference to Simon's treatment?'

'Not a lot, except you'll find his muscle tone a lot less predictable. And you'll not get him up on his feet so soon. Better watch out for any deformity of the spine, too—we may have to get a specially shaped chair made. On the other hand, it could be just a phase. That's why it's a mistake to categorise too soon.'

'Isn't cerebral palsy a fascinating condition, Sheena?'

'Sure—if you can forget what it all means to the child,' Sheena retorted crisply.

Jane looked horrified. 'Oh, Sheena! I didn't mean——'

'I know—take no notice. I'm just a wee bit crabbit this morning, I guess.'

'You feel things too much for your own good, Sheena.'

Sheena knew that. Yet how not to when you dealt day in and day out with delightful children whom you could help, but could never make whole, because fate had dealt them such a rotten hand to start with? 'I'd better get on,' she said. 'I've still got several more children to treat, and I also promised to treat Kelly Morrison before lunch.'

Matt emerged from the doctors' room a mere second before Sheena reached it. He stood grinning down at her and barring the way. With lots of people about, but no sign of a besotted Poppy to be bamboozled, Sheena went for a dignified professionalism. 'I've managed to relax Kelly quite a bit, Doctor, but it'll not last very long, unfortunately, so I've arranged to treat her again this afternoon and also to spend some time with those nurses who aren't familiar with the techniques— to get continuity around the clock.'

The grin faded, giving place to a startled dismay. 'Wonderful,' he said, 'but do you have to sound like a textbook? It's rather depressing when I'd thought we were friends.'

'Um,' said Sheena. 'Well. . . I just thought that was the way you would want it. After all, you're getting enough unnecessary attention from—another quarter, are you not?'

'More than enough.' Matt took her elbow and steered her towards the exit. 'But there's something you're forgetting. Poppy's attention is unwelcome, whereas yours is not.'

'Because I'm a smokescreen.'

'That too, if you like. What are you doing about lunch, Sheena?'

'Not a lot—I'm a bit pushed for time.'

'I knew you'd say that. Come on.'

'Where to?'

'The centre—via the car park.'

'I see,' returned Sheena quite untruthfully.

Matt unlocked his car boot and took out a Marks and Spencer plastic carrier, explaining that he had shopped early that morning. When they got to the centre he would have taken her straight to his room, but Sheena pointed down the corridor. 'My lunch is in my room.'

'No, it isn't—I've got it here.'

Sheena gazed at the carrier, which was certainly bulging enough for four. 'But are you not afraid of what the staff might think?'

'Not really, but apparently you are, so we'll leave the door open, shall we?' He was grinning again, and Sheena found herself grinning back.

'This will make Annie's day for sure—if she finds out.'

'And, as Annie is the world's most accomplished gossip——'

'Now I've got it! You're hoping she'll broadcast and Poppy Menzies will get to hear about this little episode.'

'That is not quite what I meant to say, but it will do.' Matt opened the door of his consulting-room, ushered Sheena in and, despite what he'd said only a minute earlier, he shut the door firmly behind them.

Wide-eyed, Sheena watched him take prepared salads, rolls, some wicked-looking desserts and half a bottle of white wine out of the bag and arrange them on his desk. From a cupboard he took forks and a couple of tumblers. 'Ten out of ten for organisation,' she applauded.

'You're thawing—and not before time,' she was told firmly.

'No doubt you think me very ungrateful—especially when you've fed me practically non-stop these last few days.'

'Could be I just think you're undernourished.'

'Or too thin?'

'You're on the defensive again. Why? Did your evening with the friend from Perth not go too well?'

'Oh, I wouldn't say that.' Not likely—not after hearing Annie's rosy-coloured account of his! 'What about yours? I hope you found something pleasant to do.'

'Yes, thank you. I went to an excellent concert in Stirling with my oldest friend, his charming wife and her equally charming sister.' A pause. 'And, having spotted Annie during the interval, I'd quite expected that she would have told you by now.'

Of *course* he knew that Annie had told! 'Was Dr Menzies at the concert?' Sheena asked guilelessly. She had puzzled him with that and he stared at her, nonplussed. 'Because, if not, the sooner Annie gets busy with her story the better. Then Poppy will know you've got more than one smokescreen to your bow.'

Comprehension dawned in Matt's grey eyes, along with a spark of mischief. 'That's a most extraordinary metaphor,' he observed, 'but, as your meaning was quite clear, I'll overlook it.' He fingered his chin thoughtfully. 'I hadn't thought of Mary McIntyre as a smokescreen, but thanks for the notion. A man in my unfortunate position can't have too much protection.'

'Can you count on her co-operation?' Sheena asked crisply.

'I think so. She seemed—most friendly.'

'Splendid! Two smokescreens must be better than one.' Sheena would have been quite pleased with that if only she'd contrived to sound more amused.

Matt perched on the edge of his desk, bringing himself almost down to her level. 'Possibly, but, as it happens, I prefer the first one,' he said softly.

'Because she's better placed to give maximum cover.' Now that had sounded just right.

'But of course,' he said silkily. 'Now do sit down and eat your lunch. You haven't got much time to spare—remember?'

Lunch was delicious; much superior to the humble cheese sandwich drying out in the top drawer of Sheena's desk. 'We could do this most days,' Matt suggested experimentally.

'That'd be more likely to start a bonfire than lay a smokescreen,' retorted Sheena, having drunk the last of her wine.

'So?' His eyes held hers in challenge for some seconds before he said, 'I'd intended asking you to go with me to Stirling last night. Lorna Tait only roped in her sister at the very last minute.'

Sheena gulped with pleasure but kept her cool. 'And what an effective Poppy-dampener that would have been, with Annie there to spread the word.'

A slight frown creased his brow for a moment. 'Quite—though that wasn't why I wanted to take you. Sheena, can you not accept that I'm actually beginning to enjoy your company? Your attitude of detachment is so refreshing after Poppy's menacing attentions.'

So the independence that had first intrigued Mike was also working well here. 'Just my natural caution,' she said. 'But I'll try to be less suspicious in future.'

'Now that calls for a celebration,' he returned firmly. 'What are you doing tomorrow night?'

'Not a thing.'

His eyes widened in mock surprise. 'No visiting friends from Perth or elsewhere?'

'Not a single one.'

'Then I'll pick you up at seven,' he said, just as his phone began to ring.

'And where the heck have you been?' asked Annie the minute Sheena opened her office door. She and Moira were there as usual, having their lunch.

'Over in the hospital—treating Kelly Morrison,' Sheena returned, thinking how lucky it was that her room faced outwards, on to the main road. No way could Annie have known she'd been in the building this past half-hour.

'And how is she?' asked Moira promptly.

Sheena gave her the latest news while she filled the kettle and plugged it in. 'And how is little Derek Gibson doing?' Moira asked next, naming the child they had both seen for the first time on Monday afternoon.

Annie pouted. 'If you two are going all technical then I'm off,' she decided, leaving them to their discussion. Or so she thought.

But the minute Annie was out of the room, Moira said, 'It's all right, Sheena. Annie didn't see.'

'But you did,' guessed Sheena. Moira's room was directly across the corridor from hers, giving a panoramic view of the grounds between here and the hospital.

'You and Dr Driscoll would have lots to discuss,' supposed Moira tactfully. Then she spoiled it by saying slyly, 'Over lunch. Out of that carrier bag.'

Sheena dropped into a chair and gazed at her friend. 'Are you psychic, or what?'

'No, just observant—the way I was trained to be. Matt Driscoll wasn't the only early-bird shopper in Marks this morning. I popped in there myself.'

'I don't know what to say,' said Sheena faintly.

The kettle boiled and Moira rose to make coffee. 'Then just keep quiet until you've worked out a good story.' She handed a steaming mug to Sheena. 'Meanwhile, you haven't told me what you did make of Derek Gibson.'

Sheena was glad to get back on familiar ground. 'Developmental delay, of course; slow to reach his physical milestones, due largely to his low muscle tone. In other words, he's the typical floppy baby. Now it's your turn—and, if I'm not mistaken, you've got a similar story to tell.'

'You've guessed it. He's a charming, happy wee soul, but I've put his mental age at barely half his real age. That's not to say he'll not catch up—at least partly, given plenty of stimulation. I got the impression that neither parent plays with him very much.'

'Me too. Fortunately he loves the nursery—so far.'

'Yes, doesn't he? Let's hope the glamour doesn't wear off. There are one or two other children I'd like to discuss if you've got a minute, Sheena.'

'As long as it is only a minute. I want to see Kelly again soon.'

'Promise,' said Moira, darting off to her own room to get her notes. She was as good as her word and Sheena was back in the hospital not much more than an hour after she had left it.

As expected, Kelly had already stiffened up, her little legs rigidly crossed and her arms bent tightly across her chest. 'I've never seen anything like this before,' breathed a very young student nurse who had been sent by Sister to watch Sheena at work.

'That's not surprising,' Sheena returned reassuringly. 'This is the result of meningitis superimposed on a very rare congenital syndrome which results in raised muscle tone anyway.'

'Is she very uncomfortable? Is that why she cries such a lot? Can't they give her anything to relax her?'

'She is having a relaxant, so she's not as uncomfortable as she would be otherwise.'

'I don't know how you can bear working with sick children all the time,' said the girl.

It was a thought that had occurred to Sheena more than once. 'Somebody has to,' she said. 'And most of them benefit. You could say the same about any speciality really.'

'I want to specialise in orthopaedics, Miss Scott.'

'Then you'd better work hard on your repartee. The male patients pass the time by ragging the female staff. They're not actually feeling ill, you see—just bored.' Sheena bent over the cot again and changed Kelly's position. 'See how much more relaxed she is when she's almost prone. Now let me show you how to relax this arm. . .'

The girl was a good pupil and promised to glance in often at the baby. 'Because she will keep on moving,' she sighed.

'That's the reflex spasm and the reason why she must be kept under observation. I'll be back later, but I have to get back to my little outpatients now.'

But on the way out Sheena was accosted by Poppy Menzies. Poppy began politely enough by asking, 'Could you please spare me a few minutes, Miss Scott?'

Wondering whether this was to be a professional or personal exchange, Sheena followed her into the doctors' room, where Poppy invited her to sit down before saying, 'My fiancé, Dr Driscoll, has asked me to have a word with you.'

Even though she knew that was all quite untrue,

Sheena still felt a jolt. 'Oh, yes—what about?' she asked carefully.

'I'm sure you're not meaning to make trouble, but it's very embarrassing for him to have you hanging round him all the time. But he's much too kind-hearted to speak to you about it himself.'

Sheena was completely at a loss. She had absolutely no idea what to say in the face of Poppy's quiet certainty. The poor girl really believed what she was saying! Things were much more serious than Matt had given her to understand. 'I can see how upset you are,' Poppy continued kindly. She was right about that at least! 'So you needn't say anything. But you really must promise me not to bother Matt any more. Do you understand?' Her quiet insistence, coupled with her strange expression, was rather frightening.

Sheena got up quickly and made for the door. 'I think I can safely promise you that I shall never do anything to embarrass or annoy Dr Driscoll,' she said.

Poppy came after her. 'And you must promise me not to talk to him.'

Sheena seized the door-knob and yanked it open. 'I won't—unless he talks to me first.' Then she was out in the corridor and out of the ward in a flash, so how Poppy reacted to that she had no idea. Poor Matt! Despite his cheerful manner, he must be bitterly regretting having ever heard of Craigstoun.

CHAPTER EIGHT

As THERE were no new absentees next morning, everybody hoped that the outbreak of measles had passed its peak. There were the usual hiccups: children wanting a toy because somebody else had it, a friendly fight between those bosom pals Sayeed and Peter, Nancy losing her hair-ribbon, Tom making off with Dinah's gaiters. . . The nearest they ever came to peace, perfect peace, in fact.

Not the worst day I've ever spent, thought Sheena, emerging from Kelly's room after her fourth visit towards the end of the afternoon.

She ran into Matt. He was scowling, but his whole expression lightened when his eyes lit on Sheena. 'Thank heaven for a glimpse of sanity,' he breathed fervently. Had he just been talking to Poppy?

No sooner had she asked herself that than Poppy herself came out of the doctors' room. 'Can't stop—explain later,' Sheena hissed to Matt out of the corner of her mouth. Then she scuttled off, leaving him to stare after her in amazement.

He sought her out in her room at the centre very soon after. A brisk tap on the door and in he came before she could answer. 'You're a fine smokescreen, I must say,' he reproached her with a comical scowl. 'Perhaps I'd be better relying on Mary after all.'

Sheena didn't rise to that. Instead she said seriously, 'I think Poppy's going over the edge.' And then she told him about their strange conversation the day before.

119

Matt heard her out in silence, and then with a heavy sigh he dropped into the only armchair and stretched out his long legs. 'My God, Sheena, this is really serious. I'd no idea she was as far gone as this!'

'I must admit she quite frightened me.'

'I'm not surprised. What the hell are we going to do?'

He had said 'we' and Sheena had heard that with pleasure, but she asked practically, 'How long has her contract got to run?'

'About three months, I think, but the real question is whether renewing it is under consideration.' He looked so miserable that Sheena felt her heart contract. 'A lot of this is my fault,' he said bleakly. 'I should have recognised the extent of her obsession years ago— and taken steps to discourage her.'

'But you did! You took yourself off abroad, which would have been enough of a hint for any woman,' Sheena reminded him bracingly.

'Poppy isn't just any woman; she's not normal, and I should have realised it.' Matt put a hand to his head as if that could aid thought. Then he said heavily, 'At the back of my mind I think I did—I just didn't want to face it, hoping she'd get over me, given time. I hate doing so, but I shall have to take Dr Burnett into my confidence. For her sake as well as mine, Poppy's contract must not be renewed.'

'Of course you hate it, but you're quite right: it is the only thing to do. Meanwhile, would it be better if—if we didn't go out together?'

'My dear girl, if it weren't you it'd be somebody else.' Somebody else for Poppy to hate—or somebody else for him to date? 'Of course, maybe you'd rather not. Go out with me, I mean. I wouldn't blame you. Why should you be dragged into my problems?'

Sheena opened her mouth to say she wasn't chickening out, but Matt ploughed on, 'Yes—I know!—you're involved already, and it's all my fault. I had no right to use you by dragging you along to that party.' He looked at her pleadingly. 'Please believe me when I tell you how sorry I am.'

'I do believe you—and you mustn't be so hard on yourself. It's not your fault that Poppy can't see straight, the poor girl.'

'Poor Poppy, poor Matt, poor Sheena.' He paused. 'Or perhaps not poor Sheena. Perhaps she's already decided she's not coming out with me tonight.'

'Do you want me to?'

'Would I have suggested it if I didn't?'

'Then I'm coming,' she said. 'It's never a good idea to give in to blackmail and, whatever she may believe her motives to be, that is really what Poppy is up to.'

'Bless you for a saint, Sheena Scott,' he said fervently, getting up quickly and coming over to her. With his hands on her shoulders he said, 'I'm away to look for Dr Burnett right now.' Then he bent down and kissed the top of her head. 'See you at seven as arranged,' he said, and then he was gone.

Sheena stared down at the complicated doodles she'd been making on her notepad during that conversation. I like you, Matt Driscoll, she said to herself. I like you very much indeed. But just what the hell am I getting myself into?

She was roused from her reverie by Annie ringing up to say she was off now, but could Sheena please come down and speak to Mrs McCafferty, who really wanted to see Sister, only Sister was busy.

Mrs McCafferty complained bitterly about her Dinah's language. 'I know what you're going to say, Sheena,' she went on before Sheena could say anything. 'And I have been worrying because she was so slow to talk, but I wasn't expecting her first word to be such a rude one. She must have picked it up here—and I'm very surprised you allow that sort of thing!'

They were in the mothers' club-room by now, and Sheena put on the kettle for a calming cuppa. 'But for her problems, Dinah would have been at school by now,' she began soothingly, 'and I can't help thinking she'd have heard that word even sooner, Cathie. You know what children are—and half the time they don't know the meaning of the words they pick up.'

'But she keeps on saying. . .that word—I can't take her to the shops or anywhere.'

'The speech therapist is seeing her daily now she's speaking, so it'll not be long till she's saying lots of other words.'

'It's that Bobby Burns,' accused Dinah's mother bitterly. 'I want her kept away from him.'

Sheena knew fine that Bobby was the culprit. She also knew how difficult it would be to prise Dinah out of his circle when she adored him so much. However, she promised to see what could be done. 'Do try not to worry,' she urged. 'I'm sure she'll soon latch on to another word.'

A cup of tea, some more chat and a description of Dinah's general improvement, and Mrs McCafferty was partly reassured. Then Sheena was able to dash off to finish the day's treatment notes before hurrying home to get ready for her evening with Matt.

He was prompt, and in his hand he held a great bunch of salmon-pink roses. 'Oh, Matt!' Sheena buried her nose in the bouquet, inhaling its fragrance. 'These are just gorgeous. Come on in while I put them in water.'

Matt was quick to comply. He looked round with

approval at the raftered ceiling, white walls, simple pine furniture, soft green carpet and the occasional splashes of amber and gold. 'You've got taste, Sheena. This is quite splendid.'

'Don't get carried away,' she laughed before disappearing into her cupboard-sized kitchen. 'Apart from a kitchen the size of a shoebox and a bathroom ditto, that's the only room I've got.'

'So where do you sleep, then?' he asked practically.

'That big cupboard opposite the window is not quite what it seems,' Sheena called back.

'How very cunning—I'd never have suspected.'

When Sheena returned with her roses, tastefully arranged in a large bowl, she put them on the coffee-table. Then she stood back to admire. 'The finishing touch,' she decided. 'Thank you so much.'

'It's little enough,' he said, suddenly serious. 'Considering what you're doing for me.'

'Which is not just out of the goodness of my heart, mind. I'm hoping to get a little fun out of this for myself.'

'And so you shall,' he promised, quickly regaining his former mood. 'That was a temporary lapse—and not to be repeated. You're looking quite delightful, by the way.'

'How kind of you to notice,' said Sheena lightly, but wishing he hadn't added that 'by the way' bit—after all the expense of buying this sea-green dress and matching eyeshadow on the way home.

'To be honest, I noticed the minute you opened the door,' he said softly, redeeming himself and more. He picked up her white jacket from the honey-coloured sofa and helped her on with it, his hands lingering on her shoulders rather longer than was actually necessary. To Sheena, at least, the moment was significant.

As they walked down the stairs Matt said, 'It seemed to me like a good idea to get right away from Craigstoun tonight, so I've booked a table at Arniston House.'

Sheena drew in her breath at mention of that prestigious place. 'I'm impressed,' she said.

'Just as you were meant to be,' Matt returned humorously as he opened up the car.

'I had wondered if you would suggest a set or two of tennis, as it's your game,' she said, getting in.

'I can play other games,' said Matt in her ear and with a certain something in his voice that sent another small thrill pulsing through Sheena's slight frame.

'I expect that's why you chose Arniston—they've got a croquet lawn,' she returned in a light tone she was really proud of.

'You don't say,' Matt replied drily as they set off. 'No wonder I can hardly wait.'

Sheena soon noticed that he was taking a roundabout route out of town, thus avoiding the hospital, before heading north into the hills. When they passed the turn-off that led to the Burnetts' house she was reminded of his determination to enlist the senior physician's aid, but he wouldn't have had time yet. Anyway, this was no time to be thinking of that problem. 'I've never been to this place before,' she said.

Neither had Matt, it seemed. A first for both of them, then. 'Very appropriate,' he considered thoughtfully as a discreet hotel sign came into view at the roadside, leaving Sheena unsure just what he meant.

Some hundred yards further on Matt turned the car between stone pillars into a tree-lined drive.

The house was a square Victorian mansion of moderate size with nothing—apart from all the cars parked round it—to suggest it was now a hotel. There was nothing tell-tale in the hall either. A large round table in the middle held a magnificent arrangement of roses and honeysuckle, with numerous upmarket magazines strewn around it. Comfortable-looking rose velvet chairs stood about on a subdued oriental-type carpet.

'Can you see a bell anywhere, Sheena?' asked Matt after looking round in vain.

As if by magic, a tall slim woman appeared through a door under the massive staircase. She gave them a warm welcome and waved a hand to right and left, indicating cloakrooms and the dining-room. 'But if you wish for aperitifs, sir, you may care to take them in the conservatory. May I get you something?'

As he was driving, Matt chose tonic water with ice and lemon, but he insisted on Sheena's having gin in hers. 'I like a Sheena who's been primed,' he whispered.

'Just as long as I don't come over all silly and chatty.'

'I cannot imagine you behaving with anything less than perfect decorum,' teased Matt as he held open the heavy door of glass and iron that led into the conservatory.

Sheena looked askance at him under raised eyebrows. 'I'm not sure I like the sound of that,' she said. 'It makes me sound prissy and dull.'

'Sorry about that.' A couple, called to the dining-room, vacated two basket armchairs discreetly placed behind an enormous fern. Matt neatly commandeered them before saying, 'And I don't believe you'd know how to be either the one or the other.'

'That's nice,' she laughed. 'Now all I have to do is live up to it.'

He grinned back at her. 'You're doing all right so far.'

'Good, but just you wait until I've drunk this,' she said as the waiter arrived with their drinks.

'You're scaring me,' claimed Matt. 'I thought I was really getting to know you. Now I'm not so sure.'

'Mystery is part of my charm,' she declared, marvelling at the ease of this light exchange. It was the sort of thing she'd admired so much in other girls, without quite having managed it herself. Could be she needed a Matt Driscoll to set her alight!

Menus were brought next, and they settled for smoked salmon followed by trout. 'I always choose fish when I'm out,' said Sheena. 'I love it, but it's the one thing I never manage to cook successfully.'

'No, you don't,' he refuted. 'Sometimes you have spaghetti.'

'Only when I don't have fish. Anyway, Italian restaurants aren't all that good with fish.'

'Have you never had the red mullet at Giovanni's?' Sheena shook her head. 'Then next time you must. It's fabulous.'

'Then I will.' Not a particularly scintillating reply this time, but then Sheena was too busy wondering who Matt had taken there before her to think of enchanting him with her wit. But this would never do. That was then and this was now and she must make the most of it. 'I think this is quite the nicest place I ever was in,' she declared, just as several people entered chatting volubly. In the party were Dr and Mrs Burnett.

'Cheer up,' urged Matt, having noted the cause of Sheena's sudden change of expression. 'Dating the boss isn't yet a punishable offence. If it were, society would soon grind to a halt.'

'What I'm afraid of is that Poppy may get to hear about this.'

'I think you can forget that. I managed to catch Jim Burnett in the hospital car park just as he was leaving. He could only spare a minute, but there was time enough to outline the problem. We're having a formal discussion tomorrow.'

'You didn't tell me.'

'Only because I didn't want to spoil this evening.'

'No—of course not. And nothing shall.' But even as she spoke Sheena knew it was futile. Poppy Menzies was the ghost at the feast and would probably be so for some time to come.

Matt stared moodily into his glass. 'I'm not looking forward to that discussion. In fact, I hate the very idea.'

'Do you wish you'd never come to Craigstoun?' asked Sheena in a small voice.

'At first I did. Who wouldn't? But now——' The pause was, she hoped, significant. The way he was looking at her certainly was. There was no need for words.

Sheena felt herself rekindled. She leaned forward and whispered, 'It has to be better for Poppy herself to move on. So making sure she doesn't isn't purely selfish. Don't think it.'

'You're quite right—and I know you are.' A brief spasm of pain flickered on his face for an instant. 'There's something else. Poppy's isn't the first career I've been indirectly responsible for blighting.'

'Now you're being over-scrupulous, Matt. You're not blighting Poppy's career; I happen to know for a fact that she was planning to move on—until you came. And only a moment ago you agreed it would be better for her if she did. She's got to get away from you if she's ever to conquer this awful obsession.'

'You have such a wonderful talent for saying the

right thing, Sheena,' Matt said fervently, his expression shades lighter.

'You didn't always think that,' she reminded him, to redirect his train of thought.

She succeeded. 'You resented me for not being your beloved Dr Ferguson—and you showed it. And I was hell-bent on making sure you knew who was boss.'

'Which I certainly do,' she returned demurely. 'Why else would I be here now? I'm so much in awe of you that I didn't dare refuse.'

'Believe that and I'll believe anything,' he said. 'So that's guile and blarney to be added to your bewildering list of characteristics.'

A discreet cough beside them and the waiter respectfully intoned that their table was ready.

The dining-room was the first slight departure from the country-house image. The small tables were the give-away, but the furnishings were sumptuous and the tables placed cleverly in small alcoves and window recesses to ensure maximum privacy.

After the trout a bewildering display of desserts was brought. Sheena went for strawberry cheesecake, but Matt bypassed them all in favour of a savoury. 'I'm watching my figure,' he said drolly.

So was Sheena; discreetly, of course. And she couldn't see a thing wrong with it. 'Perhaps I should watch mine too,' she said. The cheesecake was practically hidden by a great mound of whipped cream.

'No need—I'm doing that for you,' returned Matt wickedly, proceeding to survey most carefully all that he could see of her. 'All quite perfect,' he reported.

'You're much too kind,' breathed Sheena with exaggerated admiration, just to let him see how much in control she was. Or, rather, as a cover for the fact that she actually wasn't. Neither David nor Mike had come within a mile of making her as light-headed as she was now.

Another hour passed as they lingered over coffee, while the sparkling intimacy between them grew steadily. Poppy and the Burnetts—wherever had they got to?—were all forgotten.

'Let's stroll down to the loch,' Matt suggested softly when Sheena had collected her jacket from the cloakroom.

The soft night air was heavy with the scent of roses. Great banks of them were heaped up beside the winding path. Tiny, timid night-time creatures scurried in the undergrowth, and somewhere an owl hooted. Moonbeams danced on the surface of the loch. 'What a perfect place,' breathed Sheena, utterly enchanted.

'Not only the place is perfect,' whispered Matt as his arms went round her. His first kiss at that party had been exciting enough, but this was electrifying. Sheena responded eagerly, evoking a greater response from him. When at last they broke apart she leaned against him, eyes closed in surrender. Until her natural caution prompted her to ask unsteadily, 'So whom are we supposed to be deceiving now?'

Matt drew in his breath on a sharp hiss. 'Don't spoil things,' he muttered, blocking any further unwelcome utterances with more kisses. It was a very long time since Sheena had felt so little in control. She knew exactly where this was leading and she didn't care a damn!

It was Matt who called a halt. Reluctantly he slackened his hold on her, muttering with an attempt at humour, 'Can you imagine what old Ma Burnett would make of this?'

'Only too well,' she breathed in answer, not sure whether or not she wanted this breathing-space. Matt wanted her—she felt sure of that now—but on what basis? Perhaps she ought to know before going over the edge. One-night stands had never been her scene.

One last kiss and they strolled back to the house, Matt's arm around her waist and her head against his arm. He was too tall for her to rest her head on his shoulder. Anyway, that only gave a girl a crick in the neck when walking.

They spoke little on the homeward journey, but then, there was no need for words with this palpable accord between them. Now and again Matt reached across to touch Sheena's hands lying in her lap. Her mind was busy with the possible scenario when they reached her flat.

'How about coffee?' she asked experimentally as he shut her door behind them.

'I suppose you couldn't make that tea, could you?' he asked. 'I'm rather thirsty.' And he wasn't even looking at that cupboard she had told him converted to a bed. Sheena was glad she wasn't to be rushed. 'Nothing simpler,' she declared as she dropped her jacket on to a chair and disappeared into the kitchen.

Matt followed, pausing in the doorway when he saw how small it was. 'How on earth do you manage?' he wondered.

'Fine—provided I don't try to cook for more than four. Have you found anywhere yet?'

'I've not been looking. When I do you can help me.'

'Nothing I'd like better. China or Indian?'

'Tea or house style?'

'Tea, idiot.'

'There's no need to be rude. For a second there I was afraid you'd have me living in a pagoda. Is it Earl Grey?'

'It is. Do I have that much influence, then?'

'I'm beginning to think you could have,' he returned slowly, in a surprised sort of way.

Sheena liked that; she liked it very much. What a good thing she hadn't taken all her homemade ginger-bread to David last Sunday. She got it out of the tin and buttered it, impressing Matt some more. 'How did you know gingerbread is my favourite?' he wondered.

'I didn't. Call it a lucky shot in the dark.'

'I prefer to call it providence,' he was saying when the phone began to ring.

Sheena put a cosy over the teapot, and Matt stood aside to let her out of the kitchen. She glanced at the clock in passing and stifled a sigh. A phone call at half-twelve could only be bad news. 'Oh, Sheena! At last! I thought you'd never get home,' sobbed Angela Duff, mother of wee Angus. She was almost incoherent.

'I'm here now, though,' Sheena said calmly. 'What's wrong, my dear?'

'It's Angus. He's dying—I know it! And Bob's away and I'm all alone.'

'At home?'

'At the hospital. They're working on him now. Oh, Sheena!'

'Hold on there, Angela—I'm coming.' Mrs Duff was uttering tearful thanks as Sheena hung up.

'Trouble,' Matt guessed.

'Angus Duff has been rushed to hospital. That was his mother.'

He frowned, asking, 'What's the trouble?'

'I don't know—she didn't say. Just that he's very ill. I said I'd go. . . Sorry, Matt.'

He didn't understand. 'But why you? Surely that's a bit extreme?'

Sheena smiled crookedly. 'We make a great thing at the centre of being friends with the mothers, so we can't complain when they take us at our word. Angela's husband is away and she hardly knows a soul in the town.'

'If you must go then I'm taking you,' he said firmly. 'Apart from anything else, I want to see the boy.'

This'll fuel the fires if Poppy is on tonight, Sheena was thinking as they burst into Paediatrics, but it was Jock Stewart, the junior registrar, who was bending over Angus's cot.

His mother promptly flung herself into Sheena's arms and Sheena held her, letting her cry, while Dr Stewart stared in amazement at Matt. 'I was expecting Dr Walker, sir. Still, he is your patient. . .'

There ensued a whispered consultation between the doctors during which Angus's mother calmed down a bit and Sheena was able to get the story.

The history was so much like that of baby Kelly that she didn't need Matt to tell her that Angus too had meningitis. The measles outbreak had been bad enough, but this was quite appalling. In a few calm sentences Matt explained the diagnosis to Mrs Duff and also that Angus was very ill, but not in any danger as long as he responded to treatment, which he would do, almost certainly. 'Sister has a room all ready for you, my dear,' he continued in a tone of gentle authority, 'so Miss Scott will be going home now. She's got a heavy day ahead of her tomorrow and she needs to get a few hours' sleep. You'll find the night nurses very supportive.'

'Yes, well—thanks, Doctor.' Clearly Angela Duff had been hoping that Sheena would stay; as she would have but for Matt's intervention.

So Sheena said goodnight to Angela, promising to come and see her first thing next morning before starting work.

'You know, I really should have——' she began, looking back over her shoulder as they left the ward.

'No, you should not. You do much more than enough as it is. Your concern does you great credit, but you mustn't let the job take you over completely.'

'But it's not like any other physio job,' Sheena sighed. 'These families really need so much more from us.'

'All the more reason to keep fit and well and not run yourselves into the ground,' Matt said sensibly. 'Now get in the car and stop arguing, or I shall have to write "shows a deplorable tendency to answer back" on your debit sheet.'

'This is worse than going out with a colonel in the KGB,' Sheena muttered as they set off.

'And you'd know all about that, would you? What a lot I still have to find out,' sighed Matt.

'That tea will be well and truly stewed by now,' said Sheena, having unlocked her door for the second time that morning. 'Never mind—I can soon make some more.'

'I'm not coming in this time, Sheena,' Matt said gently. He put his hands on her waist and drew her towards him, looking deep into her eyes. 'This is not at all how I hoped our evening would turn out. Better luck next time, perhaps.' He kissed her warmly and unhurriedly, but this time quite without passion. 'Goodnight, sweet girl,' he whispered. 'Sleep well.'

Sheena watched him go. So how had he expected the evening to end—as if she couldn't guess? But she was no nearer knowing how serious or otherwise were his thoughts of her. And men thought that being a woman was a doddle!

CHAPTER NINE

NEXT morning, as promised, Sheena went straight to see wee Angus and his mother. There was little change in the child, but his mother was calmer. The quiet efficiency all around her had been reassuring. Also she had managed to contact her husband, who was cutting short his business trip. 'But do say you'll come again, Sheena,' she pleaded.

'Of course I will!' Sheena promised. With Kelly still so stiff, she'd be in the ward several times, but let Angela think it was all for her. She needed support.

Predictably Matt ordered throat swabs to be taken from all the children, which wasn't at all popular with them. In particular, Bobby was highly indignant, making great use of the word Mrs McCafferty had complained about so bitterly.

'Now, then, Bobby Burns, you're behaving like a wee bairn. Any more of this carry on and you'll not get to help Sheena this afternoon,' threatened Charlie. She couldn't have hit on a more suitable deterrent, because Bobby was a born performer.

Inevitably all this extra activity held up the routine work and, despite some of the children being away sick, Sheena felt herself slipping further and further behind. Being called to the phone a record number of times didn't help either. After the fifth such interruption she actually ran back to the nursery, almost colliding with Matt, who was coming out of Charlotte's room.

He caught her firmly in passing. 'Fire or haemorrhage?' he enquired humorously.

'Neither, but the day is sort of getting away from me,' she explained in a woebegone voice.

'I know the feeling, but panicking'll not help.'

'I am not panicking,' Sheena insisted firmly.

'That sounded more like you,' approved Matt. 'And now I prescribe a nice dose of caffeine to complete the cure.'

'I've got no time to waste drinking coffee this morning,' she said, aghast. 'There's still Bobby to treat—and the Millan twins and Nancy—and the vehicle centre is sending somebody along to measure Michael for a bigger wheelchair. The way that boy is growing is beyond belief.'

'You could have drunk at least half a cup in the time it took to make that speech,' returned Matt, pointing to the kitchen. 'Get in there this minute!'

'I mustn't—honestly. Somehow I've got to get over to the hospital before lunch as well.'

'My room at one, then,' he said. 'And *that* is an order!' Chuckling quietly, he stalked off towards the main door.

'Now what have you done?' asked Annie, turning up at that point and greedy as usual for gossip.

'It's more a matter of what I wouldn't do,' returned Sheena, beetling off and leaving Annie none the wiser.

In the nursery she found Nancy crying loudly. 'All right, so which one of you boys hit her?' she asked, seizing on the likeliest explanation.

Howls of outrage greeted that and Bobby said disgustedly, 'She's on'y greetin' cos she's gotta plook, Sheen.'

'Please don't call me Sheen, Bobby—it makes me sound like a spray polish.' Sheena dropped to her knees. 'Let me see, Nancy, pet.' Please heaven it wasn't another case of measles!

But, as Bobby had said, Nancy was crying over a perfectly ordinary pimple which was marring the flower-like finish of her chubby cheek. 'Cheer up, sweetie,' said Sheena, suppressing a smile at so much distress over such a small thing. 'I know the very thing to cover it up with.'

'Nancy disnae wanna paster.'

'Nancy's not getting a plaster. Nancy's getting grown-up ladies' make-up to put on it.' Not too fanciful a description of calomine lotion. 'But first Nancy's got to show Sheena how good she is at walking. No, not on the floor. That's too easy. On this squashy old mat here. Ready? Oh, goodness, you are a clever girl! We'll soon be putting you on the wobble board at this rate. Bet you can't stand on one leg, though, can you? You can! Now try the other one. Oh, Nancy—you *are* clever!'

'Make-up,' insisted Nancy as soon as she could get a word in, so Sheena carried her along to the dressing-room, where Nancy sat down unsteadily on a little chair and held up her cheek for attention, her small head nod-nodding gently as it always did.

Sheena fetched the calomine, put some on a ball of cotton wool and gave it to the child. Then she held up a mirror.

Nancy stuck out her lower lip ominously. 'Come on, now, honey,' urged Sheena. 'Big ladies put on their own make-up.'

Part of Nancy's trouble was clumsiness of hand movement and she needed a strong incentive to try anything tricky. The floor was littered with discarded swabs and Nancy's face was a hectic pink before she eventually connected with the right spot. But she was delighted with the result. 'Nancy big, pitty lady.'

'Very big, pretty lady,' agreed Sheena.

'Nancy wants licksip.'

'Nancy's going to have her dinner soon and she wouldn't want it to taste funny, now, would she?'

The wee face puckered up. 'But we'd better fix your hair-ribbon first,' added Sheena swiftly. Nancy adored having her hair done whenever anybody had the time. Tears averted.

'Now, who wants to be next?' asked Sheena when Nancy had been fixed up more or less to her satisfaction.

The rest of the morning flew by, and as there was no time to walk over to Paediatrics Sheena took the car. She found Sister looking slightly flustered, which was almost unknown. Something must be badly wrong. 'What's the——?'

'Kelly Morrison has been fitting non-stop this past hour, and that's not a good sign in her condition.' Sister meant her main problem rather than her meningitis.

So there was nothing for Sheena to do now. 'It will be best if she just slips away,' Sister continued realistically. 'She's never going to be able to see or hear or sit up, let alone walk and talk. I'm just so thankful she's not in any pain.'

They shared a silent moment of grief for a small life, blighted from the start, and now so near its end. Then, as hospital workers must, Sister sighed, 'I'd better get on—so much to do. . .'

'I'll go and have a few words with Angela Duff,' Sheena said quietly.

'She'll appreciate that. She thinks a lot of you, Sheena.'

'Thanks. How do you think Angus is shaping up?'

'Quite as well as can be expected. He'll make it.'

'Thank you, Sister.' Hers was an opinion worth having, when she'd been on this ward for twenty years or more. Not for her a desk job at an inflated salary that would take her away from the cotside. Sister Marshall was a born nurse.

Sheena found Mrs Duff looking very cheerful. She jumped up to hug Sheena and say, 'Bob'll be here any minute now—and he's got compassionate leave.'

'Angela, I *am* glad.' Bob Duff was as calm and unflappable as his wife was anxious. 'And there's no need to ask after Angus, because I can see how much better he is.' His was a mild case. Thank God for the ones that did well—greatly outnumbering those who didn't. That was what made it possible to carry on.

Sheena wasn't surprised to find Matt's room empty when she reported, as ordered, at one o'clock. He had probably been with Kelly all the time she was in the ward. A note formally addressed in his firm hand to Miss Scott, senior physiotherapist, was propped against a parcel on the desk. 'Sorry, angel, called over to the ward. Here's lunch—see you later,' Matt had written.

In the parcel were sandwiches and some peaches. Sheena was glad he hadn't been as extravagant as he had been before, or Annie would have asked far too many questions about such magnificence. She left Matt a note thanking him for his hospitality by proxy and went to join the others.

The afternoon, though busy enough, was more straightforward than the morning. And then it was time to talk to the mothers' group. Word had gone round that Sheena would be dealing with the problem of raised muscle tone today, and the room was packed.

The latecomers had to perch on the window-sills, and Bobby was ecstatic. 'We'll show 'em, eh, Sheen—a?' He'd remembered what she'd asked that morning.

'You and me both, Bobby.'

She began with a brief, much simplified description of the reasons for the problem, and then, with Bobby's help, demonstrated the easiest techniques for dealing with it. As always, the mothers found it extraordinary that the secret of freeing stiff limbs lay in mobilising the trunk first. 'Never mind the theory—just feel the result,' Sheena recommended.

'Onny o' youse wantin' a wee bit practice?' invited Bobby rashly, to be overwhelmed by the response. 'Eh, watch it,' he warned his mother, who was first in the queue. 'Dinnae lynch us, for Gawd's sake.'

'It's very kind of Bobby to offer, but every child is different, so I'd need to see you each with your own child,' cried Sheena over the hubbub. 'Anybody who wants a refresher may come up any day next week just before the children go home. Only four or five each day,' she added, 'or the drivers will go on strike. I'm sure Connie'll not mind taking names.' It was a safe bet that it was Connie's energetic advertising which had resulted in this record attendance.

As always, the questions flowed freely, and Sheena soon lost track of time. So, it seemed, did the mothers, keeping up a steady barrage. And then a hush fell on the group, and in the unexpected silence Matt stepped into the room. 'Does anybody have a question for me?' he offered, but they were all too shy. 'Well, then, do you mind if I steal Miss Scott away from you now?'

Naturally everybody murmured agreement, so Sheena said good evening and stepped outside with Matt. 'The door wasn't quite shut and I was listening for quite a while,' he said. 'You certainly know how to put things in a way they can easily grasp. I've only got one criticism to make.'

'Oh, yes—and what is it?'

'The amount of overtime you put in. Do you realise it's almost seven?'

'It can't be!'

'I assure you, it is.'

'Then you're putting in some extra time yourself.'

'If you really want to know, I've been hanging round waiting for you for the past half-hour.'

'I'm very flattered,' said Sheena, dimpling.

'And so you should be! Now get changed as quickly as you can and meet me by the car.'

'Yes, sir—right away, sir,' she returned meekly for the benefit of the mothers streaming past them now on their way out.

As they drove away five minutes later Sheena said, 'I'd have expected you to play tennis tonight in such gorgeous weather.'

'I'd intended to—until I thought of something better to do.' His sidelong glance was provocative.

'Don't get carried away—remember you're on call.'

'Thanks for the cold shower—it's just what I needed,' returned Matt satirically as he stopped the car outside a block of roomy pre-war flats that fronted Craigstoun's main park, little more than three minutes' drive from the hospital.

'Park Mansions,' Sheena commented unnecessarily. 'Is this where you're staying, or are we paying a domiciliary visit to a patient?'

'No wonder you're not married,' considered Matt. 'That quick tongue of yours would terrify the average male.'

'It doesn't seem to be terrifying you.'

'No it doesn't, but then, I'm not the average male,'

he said in a very superior way that would have been infuriating if it hadn't so obviously been a put-on. 'To continue. My parents live here, but they're away visiting my sister in New Zealand, and right now I'm inviting you to share a supper of cold Tay salmon.'

'And I'm accepting—though I probably wouldn't for anything less!'

'Thank goodness I didn't suggest kippers, then,' Matt returned drily. 'Now be so good as to smile at anybody we happen to meet, will you? I wouldn't want it thought I was trying to smuggle you in. This is a very respectable establishment.'

'Neither would I,' declared Sheena very firmly, to be answered with a glance of wry amusement. How easy he was to talk to now. And how much she enjoyed their smart exchanges. She'd never known anything like this before.

The Driscoll flat was on the first floor, looking south over the park. The sitting-room was large and quietly comfortable, with plenty of armchairs, a large roll-top desk and a small upright piano. 'My father was a banker and my mother taught music,' said Matt in explanation.

'But you chose medicine.'

'So did my sister, but we've both inherited our mother's love of music.'

Sheena could have guessed that, remembering Annie's account of the Stirling sighting. Matt had strolled over to a small side-table between the windows. 'Will you have a sherry?' he asked.

'Just a small one would be lovely. I've not eaten since that delicious lunch you so thoughtfully provided. You're keeping it up, aren't you?'

'What?'

'Feeding me.'

'So how else does one entertain a girl in this benighted place?'

Sheena said slyly, 'There's always the Golden Mecca disco.'

'Sounds more like the Fiery Hell to me,' said Matt dismissively as he poured two sherries. He handed one to Sheena. 'Bring that out to the kitchen and help me to make a salad.'

In the kitchen he produced an extravagant variety of ingredients from the fridge, then grinned lop-sidedly at Sheena. 'Left to myself, it'd likely be a couple of tomatoes and a dollop of bought-in coleslaw.'

'Yet you bought all this lot. How could you be sure I'd come tonight?'

Thoughtfully he scratched his chin. Then, with a tantalising look, he said, 'I was hoping you'd find it an irresistible suggestion, but if you hadn't there's a girl at the tennis club who seems very—obliging.'

'Another little smokescreen perhaps?'

'You could be right, though I've never had occasion to test her out in that capacity.'

'Perhaps she's not so strategically placed as I am for being useful,' suggested Sheena, keeping her end up.

'That is very true. I don't see Poppy needing to consult a vet.'

'I've decided that you are a bit of a ladies' man, Matt Driscoll,' she challenged.

He handed her a sharp knife. 'That's for the cucumber and not my back,' he said. 'So how's your gentleman friend from Perth? And the other one who is so poorly?'

'How do you know they're male?'

'Did I say so?'

'No, but——'

'Are they?'

'Yes, but——'

'I rest my case,' said Matt triumphantly.

Temporarily stuck for words, Sheena bent over the chopping-board and took it out on the cucumber, missing the tender little smile with which Matt was regarding her. They continued their light-hearted sparring over supper, which they ate at the kitchen table. Afterwards they returned to the sitting-room, now transformed into a rosy bower in the slanting rays of the setting sun.

'You'll find this sofa very comfortable,' suggested Matt. Sheena sat down obediently, wondering how she had come to overlook it while appraising the room earlier.

Matt sat beside her, his right arm stretched out along the back—and very well placed for transfer to her shoulders. Which soon it was. Then with his left hand he cupped her chin, studying her face with obvious pleasure.

Sheena suddenly felt very vulnerable. 'You don't have to, you know,' she said unsteadily. 'Kiss me, I mean.' How vapid that had sounded!

'I realise there's no obligation,' he said gently, 'but I'm going to, all the same.'

And that was all it took to make Sheena completely forget about senior registrars and vets and best friends' sisters-in-law. Her full soft lips parted expectantly.

His kisses were light and teasing; an extension of all that verbal cut and thrust earlier. 'You're alluring—and sweet—and infuriatingly tantalising,' he murmured in between.

Sheena resisted a sudden mad urge to fling her arms around his neck and force the pace. 'I'm also bewildered,' she murmured back instead. 'Why do we need a smokescreen when we're alone?'

'Call it a rehearsal if you like.' He kissed her again.

And then again, and this time his kisses were neither light nor teasing. Small spurts of desire ran together in a flame that threatened to consume her. She lay under him, open like a flower—defenceless. But in her eyes was pleading. There had been hurt enough in her life already.

His eyes mirrored her own desire, but there was something else too. 'I've never known anyone quite like you,' he murmured with wonder. 'You're innocent, vulnerable—like a child. In a crazy sort of way you scare me. Sheena—what do you expect of me?'

'I—don't know,' she breathed unsteadily, quite unable to express her complex yearning—for his body, his love, for stability, constancy, assurance. . .a whole new life.

'I want you—I can't conceal that—but you seem to need. . .more time, I think. When you've decided, I'll be here.'

'Oh, Matt. . .' She couldn't find the words, but her gratitude was in her eyes.

He kissed her just once more with a forced detachment. 'I don't know what's come over me,' he said with a lightness that was equally forced. 'I think you must be getting under my skin.' He relaxed his hold on her and stood up. 'Why did you not remind me to fetch the coffee? It's probably turned to treacle by now.'

He shut the door, leaving her alone. A breathing-space for both of us, she guessed. His forbearance had surprised her, given that he had, so to speak, got it made. Such a very little more pressure and her uncertainties would have been quite swamped. Perhaps he, too, was falling in love and wanted to be quite sure of her feelings first.

Immediately she dismissed that as too fanciful. What

was more likely was that he had read her confusion—had realised that a casual affair was not what she was looking for. So he had backed off to reconsider. Poppy Menzies had given him a bad time for so long; naturally he would be very careful about getting involved again. Yes, that must be how it was and it tied in so well with his graceful exit-line. So clever of him to let them both off the hook like that. But then Matt was a master with words.

'Black or white? There's some cream left.' Matt put down the coffee-tray on the table beside her and gave her a look of friendly enquiry.

She envied his *savoir-faire*, while at the same time she resented it. It seemed to confirm that her second reading of his state of mind had been the right one. 'Black, please,' she managed with a watery smile. 'That was a wickedly rich pudding.'

'You don't believe in living dangerously, do you?' he asked lightly, with what seemed like further confirmation.

'No,' she answered briefly. 'I think that doing that requires a certain sort of luck—and lack of depth—which I just don't have.'

'I would certainly never call you shallow,' said Matt, sitting down well away from her this time, in an armchair by the empty grate.

'I suppose I rather resemble Poppy Menzies in that respect,' Sheena assayed experimentally.

'There is no resemblance whatever between you and Poppy Menzies,' Matt asserted quietly as the phone by his side began to ring.

'Dad! Sure I can hear you, loud and clear!' he said, making it plain where the call was coming from. Sheena reached for a newspaper to show she wasn't listening.

It was a lengthy call, with Matt talking to both his

parents, his sister and her numerous family, before his father came on the line again. 'Tomorrow week— Edinburgh airport at noon. Don't worry, I'll be there. No—no problem. I'm off next weekend. Thanks for the call. Bye, then.' He replaced the receiver.

By now darkness was falling and the room was shadowy. Matt switched on a lamp and consulted his watch. 'You'll be wanting to get home,' he assumed.

'Yes, I must.' She stood up. 'Thanks for a lovely supper—I really enjoyed it. Hope your weekend's not too hectic——' She was halfway to the door.

'Hold on,' he said. 'I'm not letting you walk back to the hospital at this time of night.'

'It's barely eleven.'

'Just the right time for all the drunks to be about.'

'I don't want to trouble you. . .' Was this really how far back they had retreated?

'It's no trouble; I always intended going back to take another look at Kelly.'

At the hospital he parked by her car and waited until she'd unlocked it and got in. He kept a hold on the door and asked, 'Any exciting plans for the weekend?'

'I'm going to Edinburgh tomorrow to visit—relatives.' Just the one, an elderly aunt in a nursing home.

'That sounds harmless enough,' he reckoned. 'What about Sunday?'

'Oh, this and that—nothing special.' Nothing at all would have been nearer the mark.

'It's good to know you'll not be living it up too much while I'm slaving away here,' he said. 'Do you ever work weekends, by the way?'

'I'm on the hospital rota, and working the one after this, as it happens.'

'When I shall be off. Maybe we should try and

synchronise things better,' he said—unconvincingly, to her anxious ears.

He's just trying to let me down lightly, she decided as, with a final casual 'goodnight', Matt closed the car door and walked away.

CHAPTER TEN

As SHEENA reached Edinburgh next day a rare summer thunderstorm broke overhead. As she was caught up in a slow-moving crocodile of traffic, the journey across the city took almost an hour, with rain sluicing down the windows all the time. She was late, though not that it mattered, with Great-Aunt Agnes now totally disorientated. Dutifully Sheena sat a full hour with her demented relative, and when the old lady eventually nodded off she went to get a non-progress report from the nursing home's matron. She then made a note in her diary of the things Matron said were needed, and left.

By then the rain had stopped and Edinburgh was bathed in shimmering sunlight under a sky of vivid blue. Sheena decided she might as well try for a parking place and do the shops if successful. Amazingly she found a free meter just off Princes Street, and spent an expensive hour or so in Jenner's.

When she got home a little after six her phone was ringing. She snatched it up and answered eagerly, unable to keep the excitement out of her voice. But it wasn't Matt—it was David. 'This is the third time I've rung you today,' he said.

'I've been to Edinburgh—to see my old aunt.'

He wasn't interested. 'It means having to keep bothering the farm folk, as I don't have a phone of my own.'

'Please give them my apologies,' returned Sheena with a gentle irony that went unnoticed.

148

'I'll do that.' A pause. 'Are you busy tomorrow?'

What was this? It was only a week since she'd been to see him—and *what* a week. . . 'The thing is,' he said, cutting across her thoughts, 'they—the Frasers, that is—will be passing through Craigstoun tomorrow afternoon and they've offered to drop me off at your place on the way and pick me up in the evening.' Another pause. 'So that I can tell you my news.'

He's going to marry the daughter, she decided. Quick work, David—considering how you always used to drag your feet. . . 'Sheena?'

'I'm listening—and yes, I'll be here.'

When David arrived Sheena's tiny flat was full of the smell of the newly baked scones and fruit cake now cooling in the kitchen. Just as last week, he was clean and tidy—the resurgence was lasting, then. 'It's good to see you,' she said sincerely, having only just stopped herself adding 'and looking like this'. She was dying to hear his news, but knew him too well to hurry him. David liked to choose his times.

He leaned forward and kissed her awkwardly on the cheek, before bringing his left hand from behind his back and putting a box of shortbread on the telephone table. 'Just something for the cupboard.'

'That's very kind of you, David.' Sheena shut the door and regarded him standing there, awkward and yet with an air of suppressed excitement. He *is* engaged and he thinks I'm going to mind, she decided. 'So what shall we do?' she asked. 'Sit and talk—or go for a walk?'

David said that a walk would be nice if there was anywhere decent within range.

'The park is only ten minutes away; just give me a minute to change my shoes.'

By the time they got there David had recovered from his initial embarrassment and was ready to talk. Just a few general exchanges at first, but when they reached the ornamental lake, where groups of laughing children were feeding the ducks, he suddenly burst out with, 'I've sold the book.'

'You've. . .? But David, that's marvellous. How on earth did you finish it so quickly?'

'I haven't. They've accepted it on three chapters and a synopsis.'

I hope to heaven he's got the staying power to see this through, thought Sheena in the instant before he said, 'They say it'll be a sell-out.'

'Tell me all about it,' she said eagerly. 'All I know is that you've given it a hospital setting.'

'It's autobiographical,' said David with a mixture of awkwardness and defiance. 'All about a young hospital doctor who is accused of negligence, although he is, in fact, covering up for a colleague—a slimy sort of character, well in with the top brass. Only things turn out better for Donald Black than they have for David Brown. Donald goes into research, discovers a cure for multiple sclerosis and gets the Nobel prize for medicine. Meanwhile, the slimy ex-colleague, Martin Duncan, has an affair with a patient, leading to a sensational divorce case, and finally he'll be struck off. Only I haven't quite worked out how yet.'

'Strong stuff,' said Sheena.

'Yes. My editor says I'm the modern Cronin,' David told her smugly.

Praise indeed. Sheena looked at him with dawning respect. She'd had no idea he was that good a writer. 'It'll be yachts and villas in the south of France at this rate,' she suggested, smiling.

'I'd settle for a decent flat in Glasgow.' He looked

across the lake at Park Mansions. 'Something like those over there. But then, perhaps they look better than they are. Appearances are often deceptive.' The old bitterness was not quite dissolved.

'Not in this case. I know somebody who has one—or rather his parents have it. It's extremely nice.'

'A-hah!' said David with heavy and unusual jocularity. 'So I've got a rival, have I?'

'Don't be daft,' she said, unwilling to harm his new-found confidence in any way. Especially as she still had no idea how she stood with Matt. 'He's only my new boss at the centre.'

'You mean that dear old Daddy Ferguson has retired at last?'

How many times had she told him that—and the last time only a week ago? Sheena didn't remind him. 'Yes, about six or seven weeks ago. Now we've got this nice chap called Matt Driscoll. He's very experienced and well-qualified and. . .' Her voice tailed off as she became aware of a rigid stillness about David. Turning to look at him, she saw his face was a frozen mask of hate.

He returned her look and his eyes were cold. 'So he's fooled you too,' he spat out with a venom that made her recoil.

Matt! It was *Matt* David had been covering up for all those lost, empty years ago! Sheena put out a hand and grabbed his sleeve, feeling she was going to faint. 'You never said—who it was. . . I didn't know—oh, David, I'm so sorry.' But sorry for him—or for herself?

David, of course, was in no doubt. 'It's all right, Sheena—you couldn't know. But what a good thing you found out. You'll leave that place—you must! Give in your notice tomorrow. Take leave—report sick—anything, but get away!' He was nearly frantic with anxiety.

'But he can't do me any harm—professionally,' she added sadly.

'I wouldn't bank on it. Matt Driscoll is evil, Sheena.'

Well, he must be, mustn't he—letting David take the blame for his error? Yet Sheena found herself wanting to defend him. But—could she? 'He can't do me any harm,' she repeated bleakly. 'Not now that I— I know.'

But all the way back to the flat David continued urging Sheena to leave Craigstoun General. And then he swore her to secrecy. 'If he knew who you were— that you're such a good friend of mine—there's no telling what he might do!'

Sheena couldn't quite follow that. Were he to find out that Sheena knew the truth of that shameful affair how else *could* Matt react, except with shame and embarrassment?

But David continued to insist and she was too stunned—too shattered to think clearly. 'I certainly wouldn't want to speak to him about it,' she admitted quite truthfully at last.

That answer seemed to satisfy David and he relaxed noticeably afterwards. In a kind of daze, Sheena made tea and buttered scones. Somehow she got through the rest of David's visit without his noticing anything unusual about her, but it was the greatest relief when he left.

Then, miserable and unutterably weary, Sheena kicked off her shoes, lay down on the settee and closed her eyes. Just when she'd hoped and believed that her life could be on the up-turn, she'd been dashed down to the depths again. Matt Driscoll was the man who had all but destroyed David. She had to repeat that over and over to herself before she could take it in. What finally convinced her was remembering something he had said when talking of Poppy that night at Arniston. Why, he had virtually admitted it! "Poppy's isn't the only career I've been indirectly responsible for blighting,' he had said.

First instincts were best. She had disliked Matt Driscoll on sight—what a pity she'd ever changed her mind. But she had let him talk her round, in order to use her cynically in his battle with Poppy Menzies. She'd seen through that to begin with, and still allowed herself to be bamboozled to the point where. . .

Her mind's video reran yesterday evening with merciless clarity. Only Matt's astute character-reading and fear of entrapment had saved her. He had read her aright for a serious, sensitive girl who couldn't play the sex game the way he would like. And he had drawn back.

Only a scoundrel could have stayed silent and let David take the blame for his mistake. Ergo, Matt Driscoll was a scoundrel. He was plausible too. How else could he have deceived the authorities, bewitched an intelligent woman like Poppy—and me?

Yes, first instincts were best. She'd not be ignoring them in future.

Sheena had no idea how long she lay there, wrapped in such dark thoughts, but eventually she was roused by the shrilling of the doorbell. Listlessly she got up and padded across the room to answer it.

Matt stood on the landing with flowers in one hand and a bottle of wine in the other. 'I just couldn't——' He broke off and stared at her. 'Sheena—you look terrible! What's the matter? Are you ill?'

His last words gave her her excuse. 'I've got a fearful headache.' Not exactly untrue. 'A migraine,' she embroidered. 'I get them from time to time.' At least twice.

He came in, pushed the door shut with his shoulder, put his offerings beside David's and then eased her gently into the nearest armchair. 'Have you taken anything for it?' he asked solicitously.

'Nothing. I just—sort of hope it'll go away.'

'There's some new stuff out,' he said in the same gentle way. 'Obviously I haven't got any with me, but it'll only take a few minutes to get some.' He went over to the window and drew the curtains against the setting sun, reducing the light to a peaceful glow. Then he went to the cupboard and pulled down her bed. 'I'll be fifteen minutes at the most,' he said. 'Get into bed while I'm gone. And don't look so horrified. You know it makes sense.' He bent and kissed her gently on the lips.

Stunned by shock, bewildered by apparently genuine concern, Sheena responded.

Matt picked up her handbag and opened it. 'I'm taking your keys, dear,' he said. 'Then you'll not need to get up again to let me in.'

Because the doctor in him was so obviously uppermost in him at that moment—and because doing what she was told was the best way of getting rid of him—Sheena undressed and got into bed, leaving her clothes piled untidily on a chair.

Well within the specified time Matt was back and sitting on Sheena's bed, holding a glass of water in one hand and two small white tablets in a teaspoon in the other. 'If these don't knock you out for at least two hours then I'm a Dutchman,' he said soothingly.

No, he wasn't a Dutchman—he was a thoroughly bad lot. She must remember that. Sheena eyed the tablets suspiciously, decided he could have no possible reason for poisoning her, and swallowed them. Then she lay down again. 'That's my girl,' Matt said, stroking her hair as tenderly as any nurse. Then he gave her one of his beguiling kisses, before whispering, 'You'll soon be feeling better now, little one.'

When Sheena awoke the room was dark. Well, not quite. In the far corner a single lamp was lit, thoughtfully screened on her side with a teatowel. By the dim light she made out Matt, sprawled in a chair and reading.

Looking at the luminous display on her clock-radio, she saw it was almost midnight. Her headache had almost gone, she was thinking more clearly, and Sheena was suspicious. Cautiously she sat up and swung her legs over the side of the bed.

Matt must have had the hearing of a lynx, because he laid aside his book and got up. Hastily Sheena about-turned, and before he reached her she was standing with the bed between them and her dressing-gown clutched in front of her like a shield. 'Why did you stay?' she asked in a strained voice.

He stopped, puzzled by her attitude. 'Because I was concerned about you. Why else?'

'I might not have wakened for hours yet. And it's very late and you're on call. Do they know you're here? And if they do, whatever must they think?'

'That was some mouthful,' he said. 'Before I try to answer it, tell me how you are.'

'Much better—thank you.' Sheena usually remembered her manners. 'That stuff is very effective, so there's no need——'

'Isn't that what I told you? Now you'd better have something to eat. I'll bet you didn't have supper.'

'No—I didn't. Do you never think of anything but food?'

'Frequently, as well you know.'

He could have meant almost anything, but Sheena chose to think he meant sex. 'I'd rather have a sandwich,' she told him very firmly. 'But I can make it for myself.'

Matt was understandably perplexed. 'I wasn't proposing to make a four-course dinner at this time of night,' he returned huffily. 'You're in a very strange mood, Sheena. I've obviously offended, though I can't think how. Or perhaps it's just a side-effect of those pills,' he added kindly.

'I'm very tired,' she claimed. 'And I don't think I want anything to eat after all. I think I'll just go back to sleep if you don't mind.'

'Why should I mind?' he wondered. 'Have I not been trying to do my best for you all evening?' And getting precious little thanks for it too, his expression added clearly.

'Yes—of course. I'm sorry, only——'

It wasn't much of an apology, but it was more than enough for Matt. He reached her side in two bounds and folded her tenderly in his arms. 'Poor darling! You're really under the weather, but never mind, love. This is only a little hiccup in our relationship; you'll feel quite differently tomorrow, after a good night's sleep.' He kissed her then, gently, exploringly. Getting no response worth having, he said with a sigh, 'All right, then—I'm going now, but first I'll give the hospital a ring and then you'll not be disturbed any more.'

That done, Matt looked over at Sheena, still standing there so defensively. 'You still look kind of funny—are you sure you'll be all right?' he asked worriedly.

'I'm fine.'

'If you say so, but I think you should take the morning off tomorrow if you're not feeling quite well.'

'I will be, I'm sure.' And then, because, although she'd done with the man, only a fool would quarrel with the boss, Sheena added, 'Thanks for being so kind and understanding tonight. I'm grateful.'

'I'm not just a fair-weather friend, Sheena,' Matt returned quietly before letting himself out of the flat. She waited until the sound of his footsteps had died away before getting back into bed.

CHAPTER ELEVEN

IT WASN'T until she was ready to leave next morning that Sheena discovered Matt had gone off with her keys. Either she must seek him out to get them back, or she must wake up the lazy caretaker, Mrs Marr, who kept her spare set. No choice really.

In between hammering on Mrs Marr's door and shouting through her letterbox, Sheena wearily reviewed the situation yet again, despite having gone over it endlessly during a restless night.

She was more than half in love with a man called Matt Driscoll, who owed his present status in the medical world to her disgraced friend David Brown, who had taken the blame—and the punishment—for Matt's blunder. She hated admitting that, but, since Matt's initial attitude to her had left a lot to be desired, his conduct overall was consistent. He was smooth, he was clever and he was very plausible—which was why he was so successful at manipulating people and circumstances to suit himself. When it occurred to Sheena that this harsh scenario left unanswered the question of his concern for poor, unhappy, mixed-up Poppy she explained that away as all part of the act put on to excite sympathy.

The caretaker opened the door just as Sheena hammered on it again, and she all but lost her balance. Mrs Marr eyed her blearily. 'Ye're drunk,' she considered as Sheena staggered on the doorstep. 'Whit in the name o' Gowd are ye wantin' at this hour?'

'It is half-past eight, Mrs Marr—not the middle of the night, and I'd like my spare keys, please.'

'Have ye lost th'ithers, then? Ye'll need to tell the polis.'

'They're not lost—a—a. . .a friend has them.'

Mrs Marr's nicotine-stained lip curled in derision. 'That'll be yer fancy man, nae doot. I saw him sneakin' oot in the middle o' the nicht.'

'Midnight is not the middle of the night, Mrs Marr,' Sheena heard herself insisting rather absurdly as Mrs Marr turned her back and shuffled off, sighing heavily to indicate oppression.

'Could ye no' ha'e let a body sleep an' come for these yins when ye got hame the nicht?' she asked when she returned with the keys.

'You're always either at bingo or in the pub when I get home from work,' said Sheena, which just about made the score three-all, she reckoned.

She was, of course, late for work in consequence. 'You came,' cried Betty and Jane in chorus when Sheena burst into the nursery, panting and apologetic.

'Well, yes,' she answered, puzzled. 'Why not?'

'Dr Driscoll came specially before his clinic to tell us you might not come in as you weren't very well last night,' explained Betty, trying hard not to sound curious.

Sheena cursed Matt silently before saying, 'I wasn't, but I'm fine now. How was your week?'

'Rapturous. How did Dr Driscoll know you were ill, Sheena?'

'He just called round about something—I forget what—and found me having one of my heads. I'm so glad you had a happy week, Betty, so now we'd better bring her up to date, hadn't we, Jane?' Sheena wasn't usually that abrupt with them, and both girls were clearly surprised. She'd have to make it up to them somehow. . .

All the measles sufferers were back that day, so only Angus was missing. Sharon was heartbroken about that and was convinced it was all her fault. 'I've gone and gi'en him the measles,' she wailed for quite ten minutes, and only a go on the Jungle Jim consoled her.

'The Monday Morning Syndrome is rampant today,' observed Betty some time later after battling with Bobby's stiff limbs.

Sheena had been having similar difficulty with Michael. 'Never mind,' she said, 'I'm hoping I've solved it.' And then she told Betty all about the success of Friday's meeting and her offers of individual refreshers during the coming week.

Betty sniffed. 'Bet you half of 'em'll not turn up.'

'Bet you they will!'

'What's really needed is a nursery that's open seven days a week,' persisted Betty. 'But just think of the cost.'

Then it was Jane's turn. 'My brother-in-law, who is a banker, says that if the health service and the DHSS and all the pressure groups demanding more money from the government were given what they wanted then the basic rate of tax would have to be at least fifty pence in the pound,' she said.

Silence for a second while the other two physios tried to digest that. Then Sheena said, 'All I can hope is that he's got his sums wrong—banker or no banker. Has anybody seen Michael's gaiters? If he doesn't get his walk soon he'll do his nut.'

Despite the problems and the grumbles, plus an almost full attendance, this had to be an easier morning with Betty back. Jane, as always, darted off on the stroke of twelve, but Betty stayed on for lunch. She was always extra lonely following her husband's brief leaves.

They forgathered as usual in Sheena's room and had hardly begun their meal when Matt came in. He looked only at Sheena; the others might not have been there. 'Sheena, might I have a word?'

'Of course,' she agreed, less from eagerness than to stop the others guessing that something was wrong. 'Are you returning my keys?' she asked as soon as the door was shut.

'Keys? Sorry—I must have left them in my other jacket. Never mind, I'll give them to you tonight. I'm off tonight,' he added with some eye-widening that could be promising all sorts of things.

'I'm afraid I'm playing in a golf match this evening,' Sheena invented. 'How is Kelly this morning?'

His expression grew dark. 'Apart from just wanting to see you, my other reason for coming last night was to tell you about her. Then, when I found you in such distress——' He reached out and put a hand on her shoulder, removing it at once when he felt her flinch. 'Sheena, Kelly died at four yesterday afternoon. She put up a gallant fight—and lost. It was a merciful release—we all know that—but the death of a child— any child—always seems so unnecessary.'

Moving words, if she hadn't known of one child who had died as a direct result of his negligence. 'The parents always think so—as I'm sure you've always found.'

'That's perfectly natural,' he agreed with no trace of embarrassment or guilt. 'Losing one's child has to be one of the most tragic things that can happen in life.'

'Especially if the death could have been avoided.'

'Oh, come, Sheena! You must know we did everything possible for Kelly, despite her appalling handicaps.'

'Yes, I know that everything possible was done for *Kelly*,' Sheena returned with slight emphasis.

'Well, then. . .' This time Matt grasped Sheena's elbow. 'You're upset, as I knew you would be. That's why I planned to tell you last night; so that you'd have time to compose yourself.' He bent down to inspect her face more closely. 'You've not still got that migraine, have you? Because if so——'

'No, it's quite gone. Thank you.'

'Then what is wrong? You're behaving like somebody in shock and it can't all be due to Kelly's death. You must have faced such a thing many times before.'

'There's nothing—really. I'm just a bit tired, that's all.'

'Are you still a bit upset about Friday?' he asked hesitantly.

'Heavens, no—certainly not. I hope I'm a bit more grown up than that.'

'Promise?'

'Promise.' That particular incident had subsided to nothing beside yesterday's bombshell.

'That's all right, then. So I'll come and collect you after your match, shall I? If you win we'll celebrate, and if you lose I'll supply the comfort.'

'I'm sorry, Matt, but I really cannot see you tonight.'

Realising she was not to be persuaded, he sighed and said, 'All right; tomorrow, then.'

'Not tomorrow either. In fact, I'm pretty well tied up all week.'

'You're giving me the brush-off,' Matt realised grimly, 'and you'd better have a pretty good reason, but I'd rather not discuss it out here.' And with that he hustled Sheena unceremoniously along the corridor to his room, where he pushed her in and shut the door. 'Now, then—let's have it,' he demanded, jaw jutting.

'I—I think you're reading too much into this,' she stumbled, despising herself for reacting so weakly.

'Oh, you do, do you? I'd be obliged if you would expand on that.'

'I can't help it if some weeks are busier than others, socially speaking.'

'Several nights last week you were at a loose end, but this week you're not. Is that what you're saying?'

'I—I suppose so. Yes.' It would do. What she really wanted to do was to challenge him with ruining David, but she didn't have the courage.

Matt folded his arms across his chest and glared down at her. 'You suppose so. Well, now I'm going to tell you what I suppose! I suppose that you don't want the hassle and embarrassment of involvement with Poppy's particular form of neurosis. Neither do I, but, unlike you, I can't walk away from it.' His tone grew harsher still as he continued, 'I thought we were getting close, you and I, but clearly I was wrong.' He shrugged elaborately. 'Never mind—anybody can make a mistake.'

'You would know all about that,' taunted Sheena, remembering what one particular mistake of his had cost David.

'Yes—and I don't appear to be learning from mine, do I?' Matt asked bitterly. 'When it comes to picking women I'm a total incompetent. And I had been so sure that you were——' He broke off abruptly and swung round to open the door. 'I'm very glad we had this talk,' he said tightly. 'When one is on the road to nowhere it's better to find out sooner than later.'

Sheena stared at him, speechless and angry. With his usual aplomb he had contrived to put her completely in the wrong. But then, wasn't this exactly how he must have out-manoeuvred poor David? 'I simply couldn't agree more,' she retorted haughtily, before stalking out into the corridor.

Several angry strides and Sheena halted. That scene with Matt had shaken her to the core and, almost certainly, it showed. The minute she opened the door of her room Annie would pounce, and then what on earth would she say? Sheena wheeled round and, with her heart anywhere but where it should be, she crept past Matt's door, sneaked through the kitchen quarters and left the building, unseen, by the back door. So far, so good. Now what? Now was no time to visit the wards, when all the children—including Angus— would be sleeping, but there was still time to kill before the little group in her office broke up. Sheena went for a walk around the hospital grounds and thought about the mess her life was in.

For a short time—a pitifully short time—she had thought her luck had changed. Matt had come into her life like the answer to a maiden's prayer. Life was golden, life was sweet, life was almost too good to be true. Correction. Cut out the almost.

So what? Think positively, Sheena. You're no worse off than you were before; better off, really. Matt may be a double-dyed snake in the grass, but he's also a very attractive man. Yet, out of all the girls in this hospital, you were the one he singled out. That ought to do something for your ego. You'd let yourself get into a rut and he jolted you out of it. Be grateful for that.

She would have to leave Craigstoun. How could she possibly continue working with Matt now that she knew how ruthless and unprincipled he was? A new job, then. New friends too—and yes, why not? A new man.

The trouble was, the only man Sheena really wanted was Matt Driscoll. And only now, when she knew she ought not to want him, and couldn't have him anyway, was she beginning to realise just how much!

'Sheena! What a lovely surprise.'

Sheena started and blinked. She had wandered into the forecourt of Paediatrics and her path had crossed with Angela Duff's. 'Sister says that if Angus goes on improving at this rate we'll have him home by the end of this week. Isn't that great? And Bob's decided he mustn't be away from us so much. It'll mean a drop in income, but he's going back to working for his uncle in Thurso. So we're going home—isn't it wonderful? Oh, I'm so happy.'

I'm glad somebody is, thought Sheena wryly as she strove to react to Angela's joy with suitable enthusiasm. 'You've been so kind to us, Sheena—I feel you're a real friend. You must come and stay with us once we're settled. Say you will!'

'That would be lovely, only things are a bit unsettled for me, too, at the moment. I could be on the move myself.'

'Perhaps you could get a job up north, then. It would be wonderful for Angus to go on getting his therapy from you. You've brought him on so well.'

'Any other physio in the field could have done what I've done,' Sheena insisted firmly before Angela got too attached to her wonderful scheme. 'And you don't have to worry about Angus—he'll do just fine.' Sheena looked at her watch and realised that post-lunch nap-time was over. 'While I'm here I may as well give him his treatment. Would you like to watch?' It would be a good chance to introduce Angela to more techniques for getting Angus to use his affected hand. More of his therapy would devolve on his mother once they returned to their remote home. She must fit in as many of these dual sessions as possible before they went.

When Sheena returned to the centre the lunchtime group had gone their separate ways and Annie was back on station at Reception. She leapt up the moment she saw Sheena. 'You were away long enough! Did he take you out to lunch again?'

'Dr Driscoll has never taken me out to lunch,' Sheena returned truthfully. 'I've been over in the hospital, as it happens. Were there any messages for me?'

'Only the one. Connie Burns has arranged for four mums to come in each afternoon till Thursday. What did Dr Driscoll want with you, Sheena?'

'Sorry, Annie, but I can't tell you that. Our discussion was confidential. But don't worry, I didn't get a telling off.' At least, not professionally speaking.

'You're being deliberately obtuse,' realised Annie, but a loud wail from the nursery saved Sheena from replying.

''Scuse me,' she said and fled.

The wail had been Sharon's equivalent of 'Why are we Waiting?' She adored the afternoon Peto-type rhythmic intention class and was beginning to worry that she wasn't going to get it.

The nursery nurses had already lined the children up on the low slatted wooden plinths. Now they gave each child a wooden baton to hold.

Sheena picked up hers and held it in front of her. 'Ready, everyone? Right. We are going to lift our arms,' she intoned—then broke off to say in her normal voice. 'No, Michael, that stick is not for hitting Sayeed over the head. We'd better separate them, girls. They say they're best friends, but they keep on fighting.'

That done and calm restored, Sheena began again. 'Say it with me now. We are going to lift our arms. . .'

That was how it went. Simple, basic movements, performed in time and always saying what they were doing as a way of reinforcing their actions.

After the class Sheena had two new patients to assess. Two more wee people to gain the trust of, two more mothers to make friends with, two more day-long programmes of suitable activity and therapy to plan, and two more home-care routines for four anxious parents to follow. A lot of the planning she would do at home that night. Even so, she was very late getting to the mothers' meeting. 'Sorry, girls—late as usual. Now, then, who's first?'

Some mothers got the hang of it straight away, and some never—these four among the latter, feared Sheena. But soldier on, teaching and encouraging. What else could she do? In Utopia there'd probably be a therapist for every handicapped child. Correction. In Utopia there wouldn't be any handicapped children.

The minibus driver was rebellious. 'This is no' funny, Miss Scott. I should've been off duty half an hour since.'

'Me, too, and then some. I'm very sorry, Tam, but that's the way it goes. The children must come first, must they not?' She said that every time she had to apologise for keeping him late, and so far it had always worked.

'Could ye finish a wee bittie earlier tomorrow, though, hen? I must get the wife tae the supermarket.'

'I'll do my best. You're a gem, Tam.'

'Och away—you could talk that ole Ayatollah round, I'm thinking.'

But not Matt Driscoll. Stop it, Sheena! You haven't thought of him for the past three hours. Well, not much. And she didn't want to talk him round, did she? She would have preferred to talk him down. Instead of which he had flattened her with words and gone unscathed himself. And he the guilty party! There was no justice.

Sheena continued to think in that unemotional way all the time she was changing her clothes and packing her briefcase with the papers and books she needed for working at home. But in the car park, she saw Matt getting into his car, and the rush of emotion she felt then almost stopped her breath. It's only because he got the better of you, she told herself forlornly. Nobody likes losing. But it wasn't only that, and deep down Sheena knew it. She was mourning for a fallen idol with feet of clay; for dashed hopes and what could never be. Tears pricked her eyelids, but she brushed them angrily away.

Not until she was home and fitting the key into the lock did Sheena remember that Matt still had her other set. She shrugged. If he didn't return them tomorrow then she would leave a reminder on his desk. A very polite reminder, because they were now back where they had started.

The first things she saw when she had closed the door were Matt's offerings of the night before. The flowers looked to be past saving, but Sheena rushed them into the kitchen and put them in water. Somehow it was very important that they should revive. The wine she put away at the back of a cupboard. She'd not be opening that. She took eggs out of the fridge to make an omelette for an early supper before getting down to work. This was not going to be the most exciting evening she had ever spent. She beat the eggs unmercifully, refusing to think of the evening it would have been—but for David's horrific revelation.

It was difficult to settle to work when personal troubles kept intruding. Eventually Sheena got up from the table and made more coffee, hoping the break would help her to mobilise her concentration. The sound of somebody trying to push something through the letterbox was a welcome diversion. She hurried to the door, but nothing came through. Whatever it was was clearly too big. A parcel, left by the postman with Mrs Marr perhaps? Sheena opened the door.

It was not Mrs Marr, it was Matt. He was holding her keys. 'Oh!' she exclaimed, flushing.

He surveyed her coldly. 'Oh, indeed! I thought you were supposed to be playing in a golf match tonight.' Yet he wasn't surprised to see her; he must have noticed her car in the forecourt. And those keys would have gone through the letterbox, no bother. . .

'It was cancelled,' said Sheena, flushing some more.

'How unfortunate. On account of the weather, no doubt,' said Matt, lip curling.

It was a quite beautiful evening. 'Hardly,' returned Sheena, without offering any other explanation. But then, she hadn't one. She held out her hands for her keys. 'You really shouldn't have bothered. Tomorrow would have done,' she said stiffly.

'It was no bother—I was passing anyway.'

Going where? No business of yours, Sheena Scott. 'And, as I'd understood that you would be out. . .'

He had taken the chance to return the keys without having to see her. 'Sorry to disappoint you,' she said, following up that thought.

'I'm always disappointed when people I trusted lie to me,' returned Matt censoriously.

'I did not lie,' Sheena denied hotly. Not at all—she had merely made a justifiable excuse. 'Anyway, I needed the time for work.' She pushed the door wider to let him see the table littered with books, papers and typewriter.

If she had subconsciously hoped he might also step inside Sheena was disappointed. A quick glance and Matt said shortly, 'So it would seem. In which case, I mustn't keep you.' He put the keys in her hand rather roughly before saying, 'Goodbye,' with a solemn finality. Then he turned and hurried down the stairs two at a time.

Wearily Sheena closed the door. Matt had stood by silent, letting David take the blame for his blunder. Therefore it was absurd and shameful to regret him. She might have been almost in love with him, but finding out what a scoundrel he was should have put a stop to all regret. How could you love a man you couldn't respect? Especially when he didn't love you?

CHAPTER TWELVE

'MISS SCOTT? Dr Driscoll sent me over from Outpatients. He wants to know if you've done a final assessment for Angus Duff. And he sent this note.'

'Thanks, Nurse.' Sheena took it, pushed her hair out of her eyes and stood up. 'Now, then, Michael, I want you to stay like that until I get back. I'll not be a minute.' She looked at Jane. 'Would you. . .?'

'Sure, I'll keep an eye on him.'

'If you'll come along to my room, Nurse, I'll find that assessment for you. It's only a step.' Sheena led the way. The assessment was ready; knowing that Angus was coming up for his last visit today, she had laboured on it until the small hours. 'Would you give Dr Driscoll my apologies, please, Nurse?' she asked as she handed it over. 'I thought I had plenty of time to send it across. Wasn't Angus's appointment for twelve?'

'That's right, but apparently there was some mix-up with the ambulances. Don't worry—I'll explain.'

Sheena opened Matt's note when the nurse had gone. It was brief and to the point. 'I would not have expected to hear from a parent that you are leaving,' he had written. 'Damn!' exclaimed Sheena, screwing it up and tossing it into the waste-paper basket. She should have guessed that Angela, always so chatty, would let that out.

Because a vague hint about leaving might have come across as a threat—be nicer to me or I'll resign— Sheena hadn't intended Matt to know until she'd

171

actually got an interview lined up. Then he couldn't possibly have thought she was trying to bargain her way back into his good books. Now the atmosphere would be even more uncomfortable than it had been these past few weeks. 'Damn!' repeated Sheena as she returned to the nursery.

Under Jane's watchful eye Michael had remained more or less as Sheena had left him, which was lying on his back with his splinted legs wide apart. His expression of long-suffering misery doubled in intensity when he saw Sheena. 'Ye've nae idea whit this is like for a boy wi' my problems,' he sighed.

Sheena dropped to her knees on the mat beside him. 'You've done well, Michael, but you know how it is. Find out what they can't do and then make 'em do it, is our motto. You'll walk much more easily today after that wonderful stretch. We're winning, son.'

'Och awa' wi' yer blether,' responded Michael disgustedly.

The rest of the morning sped by with its usual time-defying rapidity, and once the children had settled noisily to their fish fingers the usual little group mustered in Sheena's room for their own lunchbreak.

'I do hope the Duffs are making the right decision,' began Betty as she unwrapped her sandwiches. 'Angus is not going to get half the therapy he's been getting here.'

'Besides, Angela says they'll be much worse off financially,' was Annie's contribution.

'I'd say it rather depends on who is most in need of help,' said Moira wisely. 'And in my view it's Angela who needs it more. Angus'll survive—he's a very well-balanced child.'

'And his handicap is the sort that will present fewer

problems as he gets older,' Sheena just had time to say before her phone rang.

It was Matt. 'I'd like a few minutes of your time if you can spare them,' he said curtly.

'Certainly. I'll come at once,' agreed Sheena, refraining from a final 'sir' or 'Doctor' in view of present company.

But Annie had either guessed or overheard. 'Allo, allo—back on course, then, are we?' she asked provocatively.

'I don't know what you mean,' said Sheena as serenely as possible. 'Put the kettle on, somebody—I'll not be long.'

Matt had removed his white coat and was standing by the open window in his shirt-sleeves, gazing moodily out across the parkland towards the hospital. Or more possibly at nothing; when he swung round to face Sheena his expression was one of intense preoccupation. 'I hope this is not inconvenient,' he began with great politeness.

'Not at all. There is nothing I can do while the children are having their lunch.'

A brief nod, and then he said, 'You'll have got my note.'

'Yes—thank you.'

'And?'

'It must have been something Mrs Duff said. That was very indiscreet—especially as when I told her I was thinking of leaving I also said I'd nothing specific in mind.'

'And now?'

'There is a job in which I'm interested.'

'Do you not like this one, then? I rather thought you did.'

'So I do.' Sheena paused. 'Of course, I can't always

do things the way I would wish,' she continued, unconsciously echoing a remark of his to her on his first day here. 'Not with the staff situation the way it is.'

'A situation I have persuaded the board to remedy.'

'You mean——?'

'They have promised me another full-time physiotherapist from the beginning of September.'

'That's splendid. All the same. . .'

'You mean there is something else?'

Didn't he know just fine there was with the atmosphere between them so tense and difficult ever since that row? But if he could ignore it then so must she. 'My nearest living relative is now in a nursing home in Edinburgh,' said Sheena, snatching at the first excuse she thought of. 'If I were nearer I could visit her more often.'

'It's twenty miles to Edinburgh by motorway,' he said impassively. 'How much nearer could you hope to be?'

'In Edinburgh itself, perhaps.'

'Moving would cost you a great deal of money.'

'Not too much—if I got promotion in the process,' she answered reluctantly, because she hadn't yet heard whether she'd even made the short-list for that job.

Matt frowned. 'You've got something definite in mind now,' he accused. 'So when may I expect to be approached for a reference?'

Her eyes fell before his steely, probing gaze. 'I—I asked Dr Ferguson,' she muttered. 'After all, you don't know me as well as he does.'

'I know you quite well enough!' He could have meant that two ways.

'Besides, I didn't want to trouble you.'

'Don't you mean you didn't trust me to be objective? I find that rather insulting.'

Sheena didn't know how to answer that. There was a tense and lengthy silence before Matt continued with something of an effort, 'You are an excellent therapist and you get results. For that reason alone I should be very sorry to lose you.' Another remark which could be taken two ways. 'And, as you've admitted that you like this job, why rock the boat just because you and I are—were—unsuccessful on a personal level?'

Was it possible that he was pleading with her now? 'I'll not pretend that our differences didn't influence my decision, but there are other considerations.' And how Matt would smart if he knew what the main consideration was! 'For some time now I've felt myself to be in a rut. I need a change. And if I don't get this particular job there'll be others. I might even go abroad. Other people have escaped difficulties that way,' she added pointedly.

He shrugged that off to ask satirically, 'How would going abroad resolve the difficulty you apparently have in visiting that relative in Edinburgh?' He allowed time for Sheena to blush with mortification before continuing heavily, 'Thin excuses apart, you've obviously made up your mind to leave—and, that being so, it would have been common courtesy to tell me. However, we'll let that pass. What is this job you've applied for?'

'Assistant superintendent physiotherapist at the Baird Memorial Hospital for Children,' Sheena answered unwillingly.

'Promotion, then, as you hinted. And, as you're obviously so keen, then I hope you get it.' This time both his tone and expression were completely neutral. 'Mrs McLean comes across as very competent. Would she be interested in applying for your job?'

'What a good idea,' she said with an enthusiasm she

definitely didn't feel. Her departure was taken for granted now. 'Would you like me to sound her out?'

'That will be most helpful.'

'Then I will. Was there anything else?'

'No, that's all,' he said dismissively.

Perversely Sheena wanted to prolong this now. 'I'll let you know about any interview as soon as I know myself,' she said placatingly.

'So I should hope,' he answered shortly. 'And, now that we know where we are, I have other problems for consideration.'

'Quite, sir,' said Sheena with quiet dignity, going out and shutting the door firmly behind her. So that was what she was now; just one more problem on the list. What had she expected? Matt begging her on bended knee to remain? She smiled twistedly at the very idea. All the same, a show of regret would have been appreciated. Only Matt didn't care who had her job, as long as it was competently carried out. If only she knew whether she had made that short-list. . .

That question was answered for Sheena the very next morning when the postman handed her a long buff envelope as they passed on the stairs. She tore it open at once. Called for interview at two p.m. on Friday— the day after tomorrow! Such haste after weeks of waiting often meant that minds were already made up and interviews were being held merely for the look of the thing. Sheena bit her lip in vexation. She wanted this job—and all the more now, in the face of Matt's indifference.

So far only Betty and Jane were in her confidence, but with time so short Sheena told the others at the usual lunchtime gathering. It went off easier than she had expected. They were all very sorry, which was gratifying, but, for their own various reasons, they all understood. 'I never did see why you came here in the first place,' said Moira. 'It's quite different for Jane and me when our husbands work here, but there's nothing much here for anybody footloose and fancy free.' Nothing but David, holed up in his hill retreat, and he needed her less and less as his writing career took off.

'Edinburgh!' breathed Annie enviously. 'All those shops and discos and gorgeous foreign students at festival time. . .'

'Steady on—I haven't got the job yet,' warned Sheena. But none of her colleagues believed the selection board could be stupid enough to pass her over.

They said it all again and more as they waved her away just forty-eight hours later. 'I wish I felt as confident as they do,' muttered Sheena as she headed for the motorway. 'Because the sooner I get away from here, the better.' She had not seen Matt since that talk in his office last Tuesday, and when she'd phoned to tell him about this afternoon he had merely grunted, 'Thanks for telling me,' and promptly hung up on her.

There were only two other candidates, which seemed to bear out Sheena's suspicions of a put-up job. She had met them at meetings; nice girls and good therapists too, but neither had anything like her own track record. In an hour—two at the very most—she would know. Either way, she'd treat herself to a meal and something new to wear before returning to Craigstoun.

Sheena's interview was the longest of the three. For the look of the thing or because she really was in with a chance? Being Sheena, she had to look for some pluses, should she be rejected. She had to scrape the barrel, only the fact of this being the hospital where

David did that unfortunate three-month stint that had led to his dismissal occurring to her.

Ten minutes after the last candidate came out of the boardroom Sheena was called back. She'd made it!

The formalities completed, the superintendent physio invited Sheena back to the department to meet some of the other staff over a cup of tea. They were pleasant and welcoming, despite one of their number having failed to get the post. Then, as they were dispersing to get on with their work, the superintendent asked Sheena how Dr Driscoll was settling down in Craigstoun.

Not expecting that, Sheena needed time to answer. 'Very well, I'd say,' she said at last. 'He's extremely good with the children—they all adore him.'

'I'm sure. Everybody here was very sorry when he left us to go abroad—something to do with a persistent female who had a crush on him, I believe. How long has he been with you now?'

'Almost three months, Miss Gavin.'

'The name is Margaret, Sheena. That's not very long, so I suppose that's why you asked Dr Ferguson rather than Matt for a reference.'

'That's right.' It wasn't, but it would do.

'I knew it couldn't be because you don't get on with him. He has such an excellent reputation for being very good to his underlings.' Such as graciously allowing them to take the blame for his mistakes? Sheena's doubt must have been showing because the superintendent insisted warmly, 'Why, on one occasion Matt even defended a houseman who tried to put the blame on him for his own negligence. You must agree not many men would have done that.'

It had to be! There couldn't possibly have been two such episodes. . . 'I heard about that,' said Sheena.

'A—a friend of mine is a close friend of the houseman concerned. A Dr—Brown, I think his name was.' Miss Gavin nodded. 'But I was given to understand that Dr Brown was actually covering up for Dr Driscoll, and so. . .' Her voice tailed off at sight of Miss Gavin's obvious scepticism.

'Still telling that tale, is he? Well, to be fair, it's probably the only way he can live with himself. But the evidence against him was overwhelming. *He* gave the fatal dose and then tried to put the blame on Matt—even to the extent of altering Matt's entry on the drug sheet. And the lies he told! I think it was all the lying and deceit that really got him struck off. Matt was splendid. He pointed out that Dr Brown had been on duty the whole weekend with very little sleep, but that couldn't explain away the lies. And then all sorts of other peccadilloes came to light. There had been an episode of ether-sniffing when Dr Brown was doing a spell in Theatre——' She broke off, suddenly aware that she was gossiping. 'Anyway, you may believe that Dr Brown was no loss to the medical profession—and I'm very glad to have been able to set you right. I should be sorry to have you think ill of such an outstanding paediatrician as Matt Driscoll. And now it's time you and I had a talk about the job.'

It wasn't a very long talk and Sheena was thankful. She needed to get away somewhere quiet and think. Having exchanged polite farewells with her new superior, Sheena hurried to the privacy of her little car.

David had lied. His conduct had been appalling and his dismissal not unjust, but thoroughly deserved. David had lied, and, besotted as she'd been with him at the time, she had swallowed his lies, stifling any doubts she had felt. And doubts there had been, but by a miracle nothing had appeared about the case in the Press. She had been at home looking after Gran and, since she'd had no contacts in Edinburgh at that time, no breath of the truth had reached her. It had been easy for David to deceive her.

But that wasn't the worst of it. Far worse was quarrelling with Matt. And worst of all was realising that there was no going back. Matt would have to be as besotted with her as she had been with David to overlook the insult of having her believe him capable of such a dreadful thing as letting his junior take the blame for his fault.

And Matt was not in the least besotted, as shown by the ease with which he had accepted her coming departure. If the car park hadn't been so busy with future colleagues setting off for home Sheena would probably have broken down and wept. As it was, she stifled her tears and joined the queue inching its way towards the hospital gates.

She had quite forgotten promising herself a treat, and once out on the road she headed west with all possible speed. Shock and sorrow gradually gave way to anger, and by the time she climbed the stairs to her flat she was fuming. How could she have been so dumb as to swallow David's sob-story so uncritically? As if anybody ever got struck off without the most searching of investigations first! If only she'd not been at home in Argyll—or so infatuated with him. . . Stop it, Sheena! You're indulging in hindsight. Anybody can be wise after the event.

And what you should have done the minute David told you of his connection with Matt was to ask around and check, before freezing Matt out of your life. Hindsight! You're doing it again. What's done is done. Plan for the future, be nice to Matt—it can't do any harm, and who's to say it might not do a bit of good?

Not much time, though. Not now she'd accepted that job and would be leaving Craigstoun so soon. Not nearly enough time. There was no need to put all the blame on David for screwing up her life. She was doing a pretty good job herself.

CHAPTER THIRTEEN

SHEENA hooked in her second earring and took a good long look in the mirror. It had to be a long look; she hardly recognised herself in this product of that impulsive dash to Perth. The orchid-pink dress—so subtly, smartly simple—had cost the best part of a week's salary. That navy kid bag lying on a chair with her best lace hankie peeping out of it was a total extravagance, and the matching pumps had heels at least an inch higher than she'd ever bought before. And, on top of all that, to spend two hours in a beauty salon getting this highlighted hairdo *and* a complete make-up was sheer lunacy. Or was it? Sheena, girl, you're a knock-out, she decided. Nobody can say you're not going out with colours flying.

As she thought that the light died out of her clear grey eyes. Going down she assuredly was; all efforts in vain. On the Monday following her interview she had begun with high hopes her campaign to rehabilitate herself with Matt. She'd chosen lunchtime for telling him, so as to give him ample time for regret and persuasion, but none was forthcoming. Instead he had congratulated her with every semblance of sincerity and then told her at length of his hopes of bringing a top paediatric physio north from London. He'd have to offer a lot more than just the job, surely? Himself perhaps? Sheena—you're paranoid!

Then she had tried ploy number two. 'Of course, in the circumstances, I shall cancel my holiday, Dr Driscoll,' she insisted with a winning smile. 'I'll need the extra time if I'm to leave everything in order for my successor.' And also to restore myself to your good books. . .

'Nonsense! You need the break,' he said firmly. 'Everybody should have a holiday between jobs.'

'But—Doctor——'

'I'll not hear of it, Sheena. Nobody is indispensable.'

She had retired in total disarray after that and it was a day or two before she felt confident enough to try again. And try she did—everything! Carrying out his every instruction the second he uttered it. Fetching, carrying, asking advice—men were such suckers for that!—even taking him a tea-tray at four any day he happened to be in the place. And always reacting with a smile.

The only reward for all this effort was Matt saying yesterday, 'You're a girl transformed since you landed your new job, Sheena. You're obviously making the right move.'

That was when she knew she was licked. Hence the financially ruinous trip to Perth today. Yes, Sheena would be going down with colours flying at her farewell party tonight.

Any excuse for a party and Annie had thought of everywhere for it, from the local Chinese restaurant to the Glasgow Hilton. But the Merrymans had insisted that it must be held at their house, and their only regret was that their daughter, Sheena's greatest friend, could not be there.

Everything had been taken care of—even to Jane and her husband being detailed to chauffeur Sheena. There would be no need for her to stick to tonic water tonight. And that must be Graham tooting so impatiently down in the forecourt now. Sheena seized her bag and refused for the hundredth time to wonder if Matt would bother to be there.

The drive was packed with cars when Graham drove importantly up to the front door, and none of them was Matt's. Damn you, Matt Driscoll—get out of my head. I refuse to give you another thought!

'Cheer up, Sheena—you look more as if you were going to the gallows than to a party,' said Jane.

'This is a very emotional occasion for me, Jane,' said Sheena pathetically as she led the way into the house.

The Merrymans' drawing-room was packed. They'd arranged things well and everybody was there before the guest of honour. Everybody except. . . Sheena walked straight into Mrs Merryman's outstretched arms. 'Dear Mrs M. . .you're both so good to me—as always,' she said warmly. Then it was on to Mr M for a bear-hug before being passed on to the Fergusons for more praise and flattery.

'I have never seen you looking so lovely, dear,' said Mrs Ferguson, viewing Sheena, round-eyed. 'The prospect of your new job has quite transformed you.'

'You're much too kind, Mrs Ferguson,' returned Sheena, because it wasn't her fault she had almost reproduced Matt's flattening comment of the day before.

'Nonsense, Sheena.' Mrs Ferguson was looking over Sheena's shoulder. 'She *is* looking lovely tonight, isn't she, Matt?'

'Her back view is certainly quite acceptable,' he returned woodenly.

Sheena flushed and stiffened while Mrs Ferguson chuckled and told Matt he really was a one. She could say that again!

'Punch, everybody,' boomed Mr Merryman, returning with a loaded tray.

Sheena chose the fullest glass, even though she knew the potent Merryman brew of old. She'd need every drop she could get in order to cope with Matt Driscoll for the very last time. She took a large, bolstering swig before turning round to confront him. 'Good evening, Dr Driscoll,' she said graciously. 'How good of you to spare the time for my swan-song.'

'As the boss, I always try to do the right thing,' Matt returned, unmoved.

Another swig. 'And do you always succeed?'

'If I don't it's usually somebody else's fault,' he stated firmly.

'Quite,' returned Sheena drily. 'Your extraordinary self-confidence was the first thing I noticed about you.' True, but not the best of comments if she really wanted to regain lost ground. Don't be so silly, Sheena—you know fine it's too late. . .

'Would that be why you went on to give it such a battering?' Matt was asking.

She had to think about that for a moment; it could be a chance. Surely he'd not have asked that unless he too was looking back. . . 'I didn't know I had,' she said at last. 'I didn't know I had the power.'

'I'm not sure I can believe that,' Matt returned sceptically, just as Annie burst upon them, towing her tongue-tied boyfriend. 'Sheena! Isn't it great? Mr Merryman says we can dance later—if we want.'

'That'll be nice,' said Sheena through clenched teeth, while wishing Annie anywhere else.

'Do you like dancing, Dr Driscoll?' asked Annie, giving the boss a friendly dig in the ribs.

'That depends entirely on my partner,' he said in a bored voice. 'Now please go away, Annie, there's a good girl. Sheena and I are having a serious discussion.'

'Parties are not supposed to be serious affairs—I

think you're very rude,' retorted Annie. Clearly she'd not been slow to get to grips with the punch.

'I am never rude unless it is absolutely necessary,' Matt returned icily, fixing Annie with a look that not even she could withstand. 'Now where were we?' he asked when Annie had departed in disorder.

'I don't know,' Sheena answered truthfully.

'There seems to be rather a lot you don't know tonight,' Matt considered. 'I wonder what brought on this sudden attack of doubt?'

Sheena drained her glass and waited hopefully for the punch to prompt a suitable reply. It didn't act quickly enough. 'It couldn't be that you're regretting your decision to desert us, could it?' Matt suggested suavely.

'Naturally I do have some regrets about leaving——'

'Shared, I'm sure, by all your colleagues,' completed Matt as smoothly as before.

And a moment ago she had thought they were really getting somewhere, when he'd said what he did about her effect on his ego. 'You're too kind,' she returned satirically. 'But if you're including yourself it's a bit late in the day to be sorry—when everything's arranged.' She paused. 'Unless, of course, you've not managed to replace me.' He only had to say the word. . .

'Replacing you on the unit is the least of my present worries,' he said deliberately.

In that case, she'd been a fool to hope. And to try getting back into his good books. No wonder it hadn't worked. 'More or less what I would have expected,' Sheena said spikily. 'But then you never did quite convince *me*, you know.'

'Of what, may I ask?'

'That put-on persona! So noble—so upright. S[]
so. . . Poor Poppy Menzies! Poor David Brown!' The
punch was having an effect now all right, but not the
one Sheena had hoped for. 'So there!' she wound up
wildly, before wheeling round rather unsteadily and
escaping through the crowd, leaving Matt staring after
her, momentarily stunned.

Out of the house and on to the drive, where Sheena
fetched up rather clumsily against a parked car. She
stood there for a moment, gulping in the cool night air.
Then the sound of footsteps on the gravel drove her
into the shrubbery that divided the Merrymans' garden
from its neighbour. She knew that a path through it led
to a summer-house, and, safe in its dim interior,
Sheena sank weakly on to a bench.

What in the world had got into her back there? Of
course, Matt's obvious indifference to her, personally,
and her departure from the centre had cut her to the
quick, and she had wanted to wound him too. But to
let fly in that hysterical way! Especially when she didn't
believe a word of what she was saying. What a memory
with which to leave him! Far from regretting her, he
must now be heartily thankful their relationship had
crumbled the way it did.

Tears of self-pity welled up and overflowed, and
Sheena felt for her hankie, but it was in her bag,
upstairs on the spare-room bed. She wiped her eyes
with the back of her hand, sniffed loudly and half
choked on a sob.

'I'm glad you're capable of some remorse,' Matt said
grimly, his silhouette filling the doorway and plunging
the little summer-house into darkness.

'You followed me,' said Sheena dully.

'Of course. It didn't take long to unravel your manic
outburst. I can live with being held responsible for

Poppy's misery. It's partly my fault for not diagnosing her years ago, but I will not endure being held to blame for David Brown's disgrace. I don't know how you know about my connection with him—from himself perhaps, since you're obviously so misinformed—but I insist that you listen to the truth now!'

'I know the truth already,' Sheena admitted sorrowfully. 'Y'see——'

'Clearly you do not, or you would never have made that accusation!' Matt interrupted hotly. 'Now listen! It was——'

'No—you must listen!' Sheena's voice sounded very loud in that confined space. 'At first I did believe David's version—after all, I'd known him for years. But when I heard the story again from somebody unbiased I saw how stupid I'd been to believe David. Especially as I know how—how weak he is. I was dreadfully ashamed of having doubted you. So I tried to—to sort of make up for it by being as nice and helpful—and, and so on—as I possibly could. Only it didn't work, did it? Which just about serves me right. So now you know.' Sheena got up and went towards him. 'M-may I go now, please?' she asked humbly.

Matt didn't budge. 'If you knew the truth why did you say what you did back there?'

'I wanted to hurt you,' she whispered.

'But—why?' Matt's voice was so gentle now. He's more forgiving than I deserve, she thought.

And because it was too late for pride she told him the truth. 'Because you don't care that I'm going.' A little sob.

'How do you know that?' he asked softly.

'You've made it plain enough. By your attitude. Ever since you knew I'd got that job at the Baird. You don't care, so w-why are you dragging this out?' A pathetic little sniff this time.

'You say I don't care that you're leaving Craigstoun. Well, I can put up with losing you as a colleague, I guess.' Matt found her hands in the darkness. 'But I don't think I can face losing you altogether—and I came here tonight to try to find out if your angelic behaviour this past two weeks meant that you felt the same.' He sighed heavily, but kept his grip on her hands. 'Now you tell me it was all down to shame at having suspected me of such despicable behaviour.'

'Oh, Matt. . .'

'Are you retracting that, then?' he asked softly in her ear as his hands travelled to her waist.

'No—yes! The thing is—oh, Matt! Can you ever forgive me?'

'It'll not be easy, but I'm very willing to try.'

'I'll help you all I can,' she murmured, standing on tiptoe to meet him halfway.

Their mouths came together in eagerness and relief as Matt folded Sheena close against him. No doubts or misunderstandings now, but a happiness too deep for words.

Then, cutting through their rapture, came Annie's excited screech. 'Sheena's got to be out here somewhere, I tell you—I've already searched the house.'

Matt pulled Sheena deeper into the shadows, and when Annie had passed by he said softly, 'It must be time for your presentation, then. Your host and your former boss will have nice things to say about you, and then it'll be my turn.' He chuckled briefly. 'And what I'll be telling them will bring the house down! But not yet. Not for a minute or two. . .'

From the author of Mirrors comes an enchanting romance

PATRICIA MATTHEWS

Caught in the steamy heat of America's New South, Rebecca Trenton finds herself torn between two brothers – she yearns for one, but a dark secret binds her to the other.

Off the coast of South Carolina lay Pirate's Bank – a small island as intriguing as the legendary family that lived there. As the mystery surrounding the island deepened, so Rebecca was drawn further into the family's dark secret – and only one man's love could save her from the treachery which now threatened her life.

W♥RLDWIDE

— MEDICAL ♥ ROMANCE —

The books for your enjoyment this month are:

TENDER MAGIC Jenny Ashe
PROBLEM PAEDIATRICIAN Drusilla Douglas
AFFAIRS OF THE HEART Sarah Franklin
THE KEY TO DR LARSON Judith Hunte

♥   ♥   ♥   ♥   ♥

Treats in store!

Watch next month for the following absorbing stories:

CAUGHT IN THE CROSSFIRE Sara Burton
PRACTICE MAKES PERFECT Caroline Anderson
WINGS OF HEALING Marion Lennox
YESTERDAY'S MEMORY Patricia Robertson